CYBER INVASION

STEVEN ATWOOD

ISBN: 978-1949788105

Published by Dragons & Lasers Press

Carrollton, GA

CHAPTER 1

"FIRE!" CAPTAIN LEA MCKENNA SCREAMED. HER GREEN eyes never left the large, three-dimensional monitor mounted on the bridge's forward wall. The four pirate ships split apart. Even though they were faster and more maneuverable than the battle cruiser *Renault* (BC *Renault*), she only needed to hit them once. Two torpedoes flew out of the *Renault*'s digital rendition, screaming towards one of the pirate ships.

The pirate ship ejected chaff as it swerved down.

"They employed countermeasures!" Commander David McCollum said. His soft-hazel eyes flashed. "They should ignore it," the fit, brown-haired man added.

Lea glared at him. "They'd better. Our marines are depending on us!" She looked at the small base on Pluto's surface. *He's depending on me.*

"Weapons officer?" David shouted.

"Adjusting the sensitivity. Switching bands from Kilo to Whiskey," Lieutenant Sarah Dobson responded.

Lea brushed her red bangs away from her eyes. "Will that be enough?"

"It has to be."

Lea leaned back in her captain's chair. Sure, she could almost run the whole ship from where she sat, but she wouldn't—no, she couldn't. Hell, she wasn't an expert at everything. At best, her knowledge on radar guidance systems was dated. She bit her lip. Lea had a great crew. The best.

The two torpedoes flew right through the chaff and veered sharply down.

The pirate ship rolled right, but it did no good. As soon as the torpedoes impacted its hull, the ship exploded, sending its crew into the vacuum of space.

The bridge shook. Three consoles exploded, sending Lea crashing to the floor.

"XO?"

"Checking," David replied as he climbed back into his seat. "We took a hit three decks down. Our shields are offline."

Her heart sank. Cain depended on her. If she died, it would be okay. She was ready for that. But—not him. Not her beloved husband.

Colonel Cain McKenna had led his marines to the planet below to destroy the pirate's base of operations and get what intel they could. If the pirates destroyed the *Renault,* the marines would have nothing to come back to. They'd surely die.

She tapped the orange button with a microphone icon on her chair. "Engineering, Jake, get me something or we all die. *Our marines will die.*"

"I'm working on it. Out," the male with the Southern accent said.

Lea glared at Sarah. "What the hell are you waiting for? Fire, damn it!"

As if a switch turned on inside her head, Sarah's fingers flew across her console to Lea's right along the wall. "Yes, ma'am. Firing at will."

Lea rolled her eyes. Was she like that when she was a lieutenant? It seemed so long ago.

"Target destroyed," Sarah reported. Her face fell and her eyes sagged as she looked directly at Lea. "Should I fire at them?"

Two pirate ships bolted towards the surface.

Lea jumped to her feet. "Where are they going?"

"No," David said. "You might hit their base. Our marines are still down there."

"He's right," Lea said. "Scan for other targets."

Two women sat at the navigation and pilot seats near the monitor in front of Lea. "Ensigns, get us closer to Pluto. I want to be able to pick our people up as quickly as possible."

"Yes, ma'am," Ensign Liz Sorbo said. The black-haired, brown-eyed female turned toward the pilot. "Polly, move us over the target."

"Aye," Polly said. "Moving in."

"Getting a lot of chatter down there," a short-haired black man said. Lieutenant Commander Bill Walls's eyes never left the communication console. "They're under attack." He looked up. "Colonel Cain's marines have engaged the pirates, inside the base."

"Got it," Lea said. She leaned over towards David, sitting in the XO's chair to her left. "If you were the pirates, what would you do?" she asked.

He shrugged. "If I knew there was no escape, and our base was about to be taken over, I'd take out as many troops as I could. Wouldn't you?"

Would she? Perhaps. Her stomach twisted. Yes, she would destroy everything, especially since taking prisoners was against the People's Republic of Earth's policies. Hell, she'd have to line them up and shoot every one of them or eject them into space. Faced with that, why wouldn't they fight until their last breath? Of course they would.

"Multiple contacts," Sarah said. "Pirate fighters and transports."

"They're evacuating," David said.

"Go for the fighters first, then the transports," Lea ordered.

"Scan indicates that there are no weapons on the transports. Just . . . people."

Lea glared at Sarah. "You know the policies as well as I do. No prisoners."

"But—"

"I don't like it any more than you do, but you have your orders. Now do it!"

Sarah swallowed. "Yes, ma'am." Her hands flew across the console. "Entering in a new shooting solution."

"Fire at will," David said.

"Aye, sir," Sarah replied. "Firing. Torpedo spread pattern gamma three. Short-range anti-ship batteries on engage."

Lea smiled as small explosions filled the 3D viewer as the fighters were destroyed. The larger and slower-moving transports crawled into space. She put up a wall behind her eyes, hiding her true feelings. "How many people are on those transports?"

David looked over at her. "You don't want to know."

"At least one hundred fifty people. Men, women, and children. Families with no weapons," Sarah said. Her eyes welled up as she fired again. "Firing."

Families? Lea tore her eyes away from the viewer. She should just let them go. Innocent people, that's all they were. Sure, they lived on the pirate base on Pluto, but did they even have a choice? Maybe. Doubtful. Even though they never took prisoners, GIS (Governing Information Systems) continuously told the senior officers in the fleet that pirates simply took over encampments or colonies, forcing the inhabitants to work for them and, over time, they sympathized with their captors. Eventually, they even married into the pirate clans. How could anyone get that much intelligence without ever taking prisoners? Who knows? Maybe that's why the government consulted with the AIs (Artificial Intelligence). Her stomach wrenched. *Surely, not all of them can be sympathizers. Right?* "Maybe we should take some prisoners."

David's stone face never left the monitor. "We can't. You know that."

One by one, the transports exploded, expelling the people into space. The silence of space muffled their screams.

Lea looked over her left shoulder. "Bill, any word from our marines?"

Bill shook his head. "Not yet."

The transport closest to the surface veered hard right, trying to avoid a torpedo. It failed.

"What happened?" Lea demanded.

"Checking," Sarah said. "The torpedo took out their engines." She looked up. "They're falling back to the planet."

Lea leaped to her feet. "To where?"

Sarah swallowed. "The base. They're going to crash into the base."

"Get our team out of there, now!"

"Aye, ma'am," Bill said.

Cain! She'd killed him. Lea had killed her husband by following those stupid policies she didn't even believe in. She couldn't pull her eyes off the plummeting ship on the monitor. As she watched the ship fall towards the pirate base, the seconds seemed like minutes or hours.

"Should I shoot at it again?" Sarah asked. "It might change its trajectory."

"Are you nuts?" David demanded. "That would get our people killed."

Lea's eyes began to well up. She would be a thirty-five-year-old widow. Not uncommon in the war against pirates, but this was her husband—her family—not some statistic. But what could she do? "Are they out yet?"

Bill shook his head. "I—no, ma'am."

Lea glared at him. "Why not?"

"I can't raise them."

Lea felt David's hand on her shoulder. She took a breath. Yelling would do no good now, right? "Please, try again," she said.

"They're five kilometers from the surface," David said.

A single tear escaped the dam behind Lea's eyes as the ship hit the base in a blazing fireball. The dark-matter engine exploded. The blast wave emanated from the pirate base for a two-hundred-mile radius. *He's dead!* She'd lost him. If she'd followed her gut and not those stupid—

"We got them," Bill said.

David blinked. "How?"

Lea wiped the tears from her cheeks. "Leave it to the marines. XO, you have the bridge." She bolted through the hatch in the back of the bridge. *Thank God he's still alive!* Lea turned right and entered the lift. "Deck twenty-six." The door closed, and she dropped eighteen decks without even feeling like she moved an inch.

The doors opened into chaos. Marines were on stretchers with medics leaning over them. Her mouth dropped. Was Cain hurt? She moved from marine to marine, looking for her husband. Every time she saw that her husband was not laying in front of her, Lea breathed a sigh of relief. But then she began to worry even more. Where was he? Did Cain make it out? Did—

"Lea—I mean, Captain," Colonel Cain McKenna said.

Lea turned around and smiled. He was her true eye candy. His arms were huge and well-defined. Cain was in excellent shape, better than those bodybuilders back on Earth. Yeah, she was lucky.

Lea licked her lips as she approached him. "Umm—how're your marines?"

"We've got some casualties, but they're all going to make it," Cain said.

"I need you to come to the bridge briefing room. I need to know what happened down there."

"I can't go yet, I—"

Lea could barely hold back the tears. "I need to see you, now."

Cain's face softened. "Of course." He followed her into the lift.

As soon as the lift doors closed, Lea jumped into his arms. Her lips latched onto his. When she broke for air she said, "I thought I'd lost you. I thought I—"

Cain put his finger over her lips. "Shhh. None of that. I love you."

When the doors opened back up, Lea backed away from her husband. "Follow me to discuss these matters further—in private."

Cain smiled. "Yes, ma'am."

The captain's quarters contained the largest private room on the *Renault*. Paintings and holographic art covered the metallic walls. Underneath the porthole into space, a dark-blue comforter covered the king-sized bed. Unlike other ships, there were two desks in the captain's quarters; one for Lea and one for Cain. Off in the corner was a green love seat and couch, on either side of the matching recliner. A clear resin coffee table sat in between all of them. Lea and Cain sat on the love seat.

Cain sipped his coffee. "Feeling better?"

Lea smiled as she picked up her cup from the table. *Better? Of course.* She nodded. "That one was just too close."

Cain smiled. "It was close. But, they're not as good as we are."

"Typical marine modesty."

"You got it." Cain leaned over and kissed her. He picked up his tablet off the table and handed it to her. "Here's my report."

Lea frowned. "What do you expect me to do with that? Send me a soft copy, please."

"Sure." Cain's fingers slid across the tablet's screen. "Done."

Lea put her coffee down and picked up her tablet. Her eyes scanned Cain's report. She nodded as if in agreement. "Adequate."

"Adequate? I got the intelligence GIS wanted, and we've killed every pirate on that base, including their commander." Cain frowned. "You'd be dead long ago if it wasn't for me."

"As I said, you were adequate." Lea grinned. "I look forward to taking all the credit on this one."

"I'll give you credit." Cain pulled her in close. He passionately kissed her.

Lea's heart raced. Her hands clawed up his back. She felt him kissing her neck.

Beep.

Lea rolled her eyes. Just when things were getting going! She tapped the orange button on the table. A small screen rose from its center. Her communications officer appeared on the screen.

"This is the captain."

"Captain, the admiral is on the line," Bill said.

"Send it in here."

"Yes, Captain."

The image switched from Bill to Admiral Steven Lyons. The gray-haired man had a cybernetic green right eye and a computer interface on the right side of his neck. A small metal plate with three green diodes surrounded the interface.

Lea swallowed. *What happened to him?* "Sir, good to hear from you. It's been a long time since we did a VLC (Video Com-Link)."

Steve nodded. "About five years. Well, if you weren't so far away most of the time, we could have done it more often."

"The Kuiper Belt is far away," Cain said.

Lea looked at her husband. His face said it all. "Did you get into an accident, sir?"

"No, I got these put in last year."

"Why?" Cain asked.

Steve waved them off. "Never mind that, for now."

"If you're looking for the report, I'm still compiling it," Lea said.

"I'm sure you did a great job, as usual. That's not why I contacted you."

Cain leaned forward. "Is there trouble?"

"No, nothing like that. I'm—you're being recalled. The *Renault* needs to be refit."

"Sure, when do you need us back?" Lea asked.

"Wait a minute," Cain said. "That's way ahead of our maintenance schedule. We're not supposed to return for another five years."

Steve sighed. "I know, but—well, you have your orders. Out." He reached for something on his end and the screen went dark.

"What was that about?" Lea asked.

Cain swallowed. "Did you see his face? I thought cybernetic implants were only for people who had accidents."

Lea shook her head. "I . . . I don't—something's not right."

"Did something happen on Earth?"

Lea stared at the blank screen. "Something, but what? How much could change in only five years?"

"Not sure," Cain said.

Lea tapped the orange button and David's face appeared on the screen.

"Yes, Captain," David answered.

"Set a course for Earth. Engage the dark matter drive. Out." Lea leaned back into the love seat, next to her husband.

"Did things get better or worse?" Cain asked.

Lea took comfort on his shoulder. "I don't know. I just don't know."

CHAPTER 2

Lea and Cain stared out a porthole from the captain's quarters as the *Renault* maneuvered towards Space Station Ares. There were three levels along the cylinder-like space station where ships like the *Renault* could dock. As usual, most of the docks were full. She frowned. After spending years or even decades in space, she always hated going home. Lea had so much more authority and purpose when she was out on a mission. She looked into Cain's eyes. "Ready for another one?"

He bit his lip. "Sure. I just thought we could spend some time to—"

"To do what?"

"Have a family," Cain said. "Every time we went out, we promised ourselves that the next time we would hold off so we could have a family." He looked away.

"During the last few weeks coming back from Pluto, I did some thinking. I think this should be the time."

"I see." Sure, she'd put off having a family, something that Cain desperately desired. He had some crazy notion about seeing his family name continue. Really? She loved him more than life itself, but . . . women broke the glass ceiling over a century ago. Lea was nothing special, she was just good at her job. With Cain leading the marines on her ship, they were unstoppable.

"This mission was six years long. If we wait too much longer, you won't be able to have children."

"Some things are just more important than starting a family. Besides, I've got no idea how to raise a child, and neither to do you. Why would you want to give up the *Renault* for changing diapers?"

Cain sighed. "No, again?"

Lea hugged him. "I can't. Please understand."

"Can't? Or don't want to?" Cain asked.

Lea opened her mouth, but nothing came out. She turned toward the beeping panel near her desk. "This is the captain."

"Ma'am, the admiral is here," David said.

"Here?" Cain asked. "Why did he come aboard? That's unusual."

Lea glared at him. "Have the admiral brought to the bridge conference room." She looked at Cain and smiled. "Let's go see the boss."

Cain nodded. “All right.” He followed Lea out of their quarters.

Lea paced back and forth along the bulkhead in the conference room. The metallic oval table with a dozen chairs surrounding it was the centerpiece. A projector hung from the ceiling over the center of the table.

Cain was already sitting in his chair. “That’s not going to help things.”

She glared at him. “No, but it makes me feel better.”

The door slid open and Admiral Steven Lyons stepped inside with a younger officer, Lieutenant Commander Alice Michaels, in tow. Steven smiled as he extended his hand to Lea. “It’s good to see you again.”

Lea took his hand. “Yes, it is.” She stared at Alice. She couldn’t take her eyes off the metallic plate on the right side of her neck, just like the admiral had.

Steven smiled at Cain. “Colonel.”

“Admiral,” Cain replied. “Please, have a seat.”

“Thank you,” Steven said as he sat down. He leaned towards Alice and whispered something into her ear. She hurried out of the room.

“New aide?” Lea asked.

Steven nodded. “I’ve had her for a year now. She’s one of the better ones.”

“Why are we here, Admiral?” Lea asked.

Steven sighed. “That’s what I always liked about

you. Your desire to blow right through the niceties and get right down to it."

"Well?"

Steven shifted in his seat. "Earth has . . . changed since you left."

"I'll say," Cain said. "Both you and your aide have been cybernetically enhanced. Why?"

"Well, the implants are better than our own brain functions. I receive data and orders without having to be at a computer terminal or in a briefing room. It's wonderful, really."

Lea shook her head. "I'll never get one of those."

Steven frowned. "We can discuss that later."

Cain leaned forward. "You still haven't told us why we're really here. This is way ahead of our maintenance schedule. Why did you recall us? Sir, please tell us the truth."

Lea cocked her head as Steven seemed to stare into space. Perhaps he was listening to whatever was on the other end of that implant of his. *Yeah, sure. That's got to be it, right?* "Are you all right?"

"Yes, I'm fine." Steven straightened up. "Earth's leadership has changed again, and she views GIS as a co-president."

"The AI?" Cain asked. "Why? It's just a machine."

Steven shook his head. "No, not anymore."

"Why would anyone do that?" Lea asked.

"There was another scandal about corruption, a big

one. After the politicians were executed, the president gave the day-to-day operations over to GIS. Ever since, the world has become more . . . efficient," Steven said.

Cain pointed at Steven's implant. "Is that part of the new efficiency?"

Steven looked away. "We'll discuss that when you get down to Earth. Anyway, I wanted to congratulate you on your job on Pluto."

Lea scowled at him. "Thank you." *What is he hiding?*

Steven rose from his seat. "I've got to get back. Please inform your crew that there will be a debriefing before anyone contacts their family or goes on leave. Understand?"

"Why?" Cain demanded. "Our people haven't seen their families for years."

"He's right," Lea began. "That's simply not fair to our crew. Besides, they've probably already contacted their families."

Steven frowned. "I hope not, for their sakes. I'll see you on Earth."

Lea watched the admiral storm out of the conference room. "I'm more confused now than before he arrived." She looked right into Cain's eyes. "What's going on?"

Cain walked over to the porthole, looking out onto the giant blue planet, Earth. "It looks so peaceful from up here."

"Cain? What do we do?"

Cain shook his head. "Not sure. We'll find out more when we get down to Earth."

"Even his aide-de-camp had an implant. I don't want some computer reading my mind or giving me orders."

"Me either." Cain pulled her in close. "Everything will be all right. I promise."

Lea put her head on his chest. *I don't think so.*

President Anna Zahrof sat behind her enormous, dark-stained solid oak desk. Her long, brown hair hung over her shoulders and her brown eyes glistened in the artificial light. The yellow pantsuit stood out from the black executive chair she sat in. Images highlighting the People's Republic of Earth's inception—both true and, well, what should have happened—decorated the walls. Two plush red couches were in the center of the room. A 3D video projection emanated from the far wall. As always, Anna had the Global News Network blaring in the background. She picked up her steaming cup of coffee as the door slid open.

"The Senate just approved it," the young woman wearing an orange sweater and khaki pants and carrying a tablet said as she entered the room. She was a pale woman with short, blond hair and green eyes.

Anna frowned. "You didn't buzz me before entering."

"I—I'm sorry," Toni Phillips said. Fear draped over her face like a mask.

Anna laughed. "I was just kidding."

"Oh, okay—I knew that." She smiled. "Here's the bill."

Anna took the tablet from Toni. Her eyes scanned the bill. It was her creation, the final lynchpin that would improve humanity—well, Earth, anyway. "It's all here then?"

Toni nodded. "Anyone who does not have an implant cannot hold a Class I or Class II position. This bill would deem them unqualified and untrustworthy to hold those positions." She bit her lip.

"What is it?"

"Ma'am, are you sure about this? Only about half the population got the implant and this would—"

"What?"

"Make it mandatory, not voluntary."

Anna frowned. "People don't get it for stupid reasons. Some believe that the government will try to rewrite their minds. Some won't get it for religious reasons. Still others won't get it because they simply don't trust the government with a link directly to their mind. What do all these groups have in common? They're a clear and present danger to the government—and me."

Toni looked down. "I see."

"Speaking of which, when are you getting yours?"

"I made the appointment already."

Anna stared at the newscast over Toni's shoulder. "GIS, increase the volume on the newscast, please."

"Yes, Madam President," a female computer replied. Its voiced echoed throughout the room through the speakers mounted on every wall.

The image showed thousands of people railing against a police line. But these police were not people, they were top-of-the—line androids capable of enforcing every law and remembering every face. A woman with an implant appeared on the screen. "We're just getting word now that the protestors are calling for terrorism to end the global government, and—" The reporter swallowed. "I can't read this anymore. These people just lost their jobs to androids and are being separated from their families. We've got to stop—" The image flashed and "We are experiencing technical difficulties, please stand by" appeared in its place.

Anna frowned. "Her implant must have been malfunctioning," she mumbled to herself.

"Ma'am?"

Anna placed her thumb on the tablet, signing the bill into law. "It's done. Effective immediately." She glared at Toni. "Don't come back to work until you have it done. Got it?"

Toni's eyes welled up. "Yes, ma'am." She hurried from Anna's office.

Anna tapped her fingers on the desk. "What do you think, GIS?"

"About the protests?"

Anna shook her head. "No, our timing." As the former CEO of Benton Enterprises, the defense contractor that created GIS, she was well aware GIS's true capabilities. It was a nearly self-aware artificial intelligence with the capacity to learn and to teach other AIs. A truly remarkable feat in engineering. When the previously failing government asked for its recommendation, no one should have been surprised that it chose Anna.

"We always knew there would be some resistance. These altercations were expected."

"You're not answering my question."

"But, I did. We are on schedule. The only real danger to us are the people in the government and the military who do not have the implants. Once they are installed, we can change their way of thinking."

Anna smiled. "And how the people vote."

"Inquiry: why do you want the people to vote?"

Anna sipped her coffee. "We have to give the people the illusion of a democracy. It'll keep them in their proper place."

"Understood," GIS said.

"Are there more protests than what I just saw on the newscast?"

"Affirmative. They are across the globe. But I estimate they will subside once the order is enforced."

Anna put her cup down. "You do know that I just

fired millions of people for not having an implant and they will demand a job."

"Affirmative."

She sighed. "Well, I knew this would happen, too. I guess it's different planning this, rather than actually executing it. Are our plans in any danger?"

"Our estimated chance of success is over ninety percent," GIS said.

Anna leaned back in her chair. Nothing could stop her now.

CHAPTER 3

LEA EXPECTED TO COME DOWN FROM THE BC *RENAULT* to fleet headquarters in triumph, not hauled off into uncertainty. She gripped Cain's hand, as if drawing strength from him.

Cain looked out the shuttle craft window. "I love seeing the Earth from up here."

Lea shuffled in her seat. They had the two front seats on the large transport shuttle with both her and his senior officers and enlisted personnel behind them. She frowned. Twenty sailors and marines, loyal to Earth, were being guarded by three Internal Security Service officers armed with particle beam rifles. *What a welcome home!*

"I'm sure they're just here for our protection," Cain said. "I can't imagine the admiral—"

Lea glared at him. "How do you know?"

"Well—I—"

"You don't. Could it be because we told him that our crew already talked to their families? The very thing he told us was forbidden."

Cain shut his mouth.

"I've got a real bad feeling, Cain," Lea said.

"I know." He bit his lip.

Lea squeezed his hand as she stared into his eyes. She shifted in the gray cushioned seat. Would they give her another command? Sure, her experience and record warranted it. How important was getting that implant? Lea shook her head, resigning herself to the fact that she simply didn't have enough information to decide anything.

"Sir," Sergeant Major Kyle Wilson said as he tapped Cain on the shoulder. His massive frame cast an equally huge shadow over Lea.

Cain looked up. "What is it, Sergeant Major?"

Kyle sighed as he rubbed his hand over his bald head. "Everyone's getting nervous back there. They won't stop talking about those . . . rumors they heard from their families on Earth. Well, those who could reach their families."

Cain frowned. "That's not how marines act. We don't worry about things we can't control."

He nodded.

"Just go back there and tell them to knock it off. We'll find out the truth soon enough."

"What if the rumors are true?" Kyle asked.

Lea frowned. "They're not. Now do what your commander told you."

Kyle straightened up. "Yes, ma'am."

"He's just as worried as the rest of them," Cain said.

Lea glared at him. "And you're not?"

"Not that I'd tell them." He looked into Lea's green eyes. "Promise me that you'll never get one of those."

"Of course not." She pushed him off. "Why would you even think that?"

Cain sighed. "We only have one real freedom left."

"What's that?"

"The freedom to think what we want. We can't say it, but we can think it."

"And what does this have to do the implants?" Lea slammed her mouth shut. She knew where he was going. Hell, she already thought the same things, right?

Cain lowered his voice. "You did see the admiral, right? I've just got a bad feeling that cybernetic enhancements connected to GIS—or any other AI—would take away that freedom, too. I mean, who knows how much of your thoughts it reads?" He shook his head. "I just want you to promise me."

Lea yawned. "I won't."

He stared right into Lea's soul. "If they make us, like the rumors say, they'd have to make it tempting."

"I won't! Enough already."

"All right." Cain looked out the porthole.

Lea frowned. Why would the families of her officers and senior enlisted personnel lie? Hell, less than half were even able to get in contact with their families. She leaned her head on Cain's shoulder as they descended towards the east landing pad at fleet headquarters. Her eyes became heavy and then . . . darkness.

"Wake up," Cain said as he shook Lea's shoulder. "We're here."

Lea blinked. Her eyes were still foggy, trying to focus on the guards in front of them. "Where? When?"

Cain pulled Lea to her feet. "Come on."

Lea grabbed her assault pack from above their seats and slung it over her shoulder. She followed Cain off the shuttle onto the landing pad. It was almost as high as the tallest building on the base. A small door leading into a lift stood across the platform.

"Ma'am, you and the colonel and sergeant major must go first. The admiral is expecting you," one of the guards said.

Cain smiled. "Keep up the good work."

Lea couldn't take her eyes off the guard's implant. *Do they all have it?* "Come along, Sergeant Major."

"Coming," Kyle said as he jumped onboard just before the door slid shut.

As the lift descended below the platform, the walls were clear. Rockets, space shuttles, and old satellites from a long time ago decorate the parade field below.

On the edge of the field stood the museum with the letters NASA painted on the side.

Lea stepped into the hot air laced with the aroma of the Atlantic Ocean. Across the street stood a wide, twenty-story building. She sighed as they entered fleet HQ.

They were silent as they navigated through the corridors and lifts until they reached Admiral Steven Lyons's office on the eighteenth floor. The waiting area contained a single desk with a civilian sitting behind it. His short, black hair and dark skin glistened in the artificial light. "The admiral is expecting you." He reached underneath the desk as if to hit a button. An audible click echoed through the room.

"Thank you," Lea said. *Here we go.* She strolled into Steven's office with Cain, Kyle, and the guards in tow. The admiral's office had to be at least three times the size of the captain's quarters on the *Renault*. His desk stood near the window in the back of the room. The walls were lined with 3D monitors. A conference table with twelve seats was off to the side, opposite a sitting area furnished with navy blue couches and a single chair between them. Lea swallowed.

Steven looked up and waved the guards off. "You can go." He motioned to the couches on the side of his enormous office. "Please, have a seat."

Lea and Cain sat down on a couch without saying a word.

Kyle sat across from them.

Lea smiled. Was she trying to comfort Kyle and Cain or herself?

Steven plopped down in the plush chair between the couches. "How was your trip down?"

Cain sighed. "Sir, what's going on?"

"Right to the point then?"

Lea and Cain nodded.

"Well, I followed the bill through the legislature, and the president has already agreed to sign the bill."

Lea leaned forward. "What are you talking about?"

Steven stared at her, but only for a second. "You are in a Class I job, all of you."

"Okay, so what?" Cain asked.

"Well—I—the government classified employment into three classes. Class 1 includes security, governmental, and any other decision-making position. Class 2 is pretty much everything else."

"You said there are three classes," Lea said.

Steven nodded. "Yes, Class III positions are menial labor located in isolated areas where the security risk from people not cybernetically enhance is drastically reduced."

"The implant," Kyle said. "So, the rumors were true. I told—"

"At ease," Cain said as he glared at Kyle. "Sir, what are you saying?"

"In order to stay on the *Renault* or to have any

good-paying job, you must get the implant. I'm sorry, but the president signed the bill into law. There's nothing I can do," Steven said.

"What does it do?" Lea asked. Ignoring Cain's fiery glance, she leaned forward. "How does it affect you, sir?"

"Well, it connects me to GIS and all of the other cybernetically enhanced people. I make far fewer mistakes and—sometimes they know what I need before I do." Steven smiled at her as he motioned to his office. "With your record and how well you're liked by the four-stars, this office could one day be yours. But, you must get the implant first."

"If we don't?" Cain asked. "What then?"

Steven frowned. "Well, you'll be removed from the premises and relocated."

"Can it be removed? Once it's in?"

Steven shook his head. "No, it's directly attached to your brain and your nervous system. If you remove it, you'll die."

Kyle leaped to his feet. "No way. I'm not doing that."

Steven glared at him. "Sergeant Major, sit down. I thought you'd be the example to your marines."

"No."

"Guards!"

Four guards rushed inside with their weapons at the ready.

"Take the sergeant away. He's made his decision," Steven said.

What just happened? Lea swallowed. Was this a foregone conclusion? Yes, they had no choice.

"Where are you taking him?" Cain demanded, standing to his feet. "Is this how we treat heroes of the People's Republic?"

One of the guards pushed Cain back into his seat with his weapon aimed right at Cain's heart. "Sir?"

Steven waved them off. "Leave us. We're not done talking yet."

Lea stared at the admiral's torn face. That thing on the side of his neck may give him orders or spy on every thought running through his mind, but it didn't control him. Why did he obey? Maybe once you put that thing in your body, you become a slave to it. She gripped Cain's hand. "Where will we get relocated?"

Steven blinked. "Both of you?"

Cain nodded. "Yeah, we don't want any part of that."

"Lea, please. Don't do this. You . . . you don't know what—" Steven's face twisted.

"What's wrong?" Cain asked.

Steven blinked. "Nothing. Where . . . where was it? Oh yeah, please reconsider."

"What just happened?" Lea demanded.

"I . . . I received an order, that's all."

"You're nuts if you think for one second that I'll submit to that . . . machine," Cain said.

Lea nodded her head. "I'm with my husband. There's no way you're putting that thing in me."

"As you wish," Steven said. "Guards!"

Two different guards entered Steven's office. "Everything all right, sir?" one of them asked.

Steven glared at Lea and Cain. "No, not at all."

Cain plucked his colonel rank off his collar and tossed it to Steven. "I won't submit, and I won't force anyone else to, either."

Lea smiled at her husband as she removed her captain's rank and flung it at Steven. "That goes for me, too." She rose to her feet. "What now?"

Steven sighed. "Now, you're going to be relocated and assigned a new job. Good luck."

Lea frowned. "We won't need it."

Cain slapped Steven on the shoulder and smiled. "See why I love her?"

The guards raised their weapons, aiming at Lea and Cain. They motioned them towards the door.

"You can always change your mind," Steven said.

"Thanks," Lea said as she and Cain left the admiral's office. *What happens now?*

"Look out!" Major Farrah Haider screamed as she slammed into Jarak Zeger, knocking him to the ground.

A particle beam slammed into the wall behind them, spraying Jarak with concrete. He patted down his militaristic black environmental suit. *No holes, thank God!* "Where is he?"

All of Farrah's female features were hidden by her environmental suit. She motioned Jarak forward towards a large rock. "He's gotta be by the mine entrance." She placed her particle beam rifle into her shoulder and fired. "I only see one."

"Got it. Keep him busy," Jarak said. "I'm flanking to the left." Without waiting for a response, Jarak rushed to a pile of worthless rock. He peered around the corner. The mine was at the base of the largest mountain on Ceres. Mining machines, a commercial T-Mat station, pallets of explosives, and piles and piles of rock with the valuable minerals already sucked out of them surrounded the entrance. Jarak needed him or her to return fire. *Come on!*

As if on cue, a helmet with the Benton Enterprises logo on it popped up behind a small rock pile and fired.

"Damn it!" Farrah said over the intercom.

"You hit?" Jarak asked as he looked back towards Farrah.

"No, but his last shot hit my rifle. I can't fire anymore. He sees you!"

The rock exploded above Jarak's head. He raised his rifle and fired. Missed. Only way to get that bastard was to keep his head down and close in. He swallowed as he leaped to his feet, firing. Jarak's beams rapidly hit the rock pile and just a hair over. With each quick step, he fired. *Gotta keep his head down. Only five meters to go! Come on!* Jarak saw the top of the helmet and fired. Missed. He fired even faster. As soon as his finger released the trigger, he squeezed it again.

The Benton Enterprise security guard was just on the other side of the rock pile. What would Jarak do? He'd attack. Do something to draw his enemy's attention, just for a second, then kill him. If he flew around the corner and fired, he may kill the guard, but the guard could do the same to him. At the very least, rupture his environmental suit, letting in the carbon monoxide atmosphere. No, Jarak couldn't give him the chance.

Jarak pulled a thermal grenade from a pouch on his suit. It was his last one. He pulled the safety pin and the button began to flash a cherry red. Jarak pressed the button twice, setting the timer for two seconds. He tossed it over the pile, hopefully just out of reach of the security guard.

The guard bolted from behind the rock pile, towards the T-Mat station.

Jarak fired. This time, he hit his target. He stood up as the security guard crumpled to the ground. "It's all clear."

"Coming out," Farrah said.

Jarak smiled as Farrah came out from the rock pile she was hiding behind. He walked over towards the guard's body, kicking away his weapon. He rolled him over. The particle beam pierced the guard's suit and his body, right through the chest. Jarak could have put his fist in the hole his weapon left. Yeah, he was dead.

Farrah tapped Jarak on the shoulder. "Look!"

People wearing gray environmental suits started coming out of the mine. Their helmets had a clear face, showing their euphoria. They were human colonists, miners for Benton Enterprises. A woman stepped forward, heading directly toward Jarak.

"Major, check in with the other teams. Also, call up to the *Courage* and find out if there are any signs of reinforcements," Jarak said.

"Yes, sir," Farrah replied.

The woman smiled as she approached Jarak. "I can't thank you enough. I'm Janet."

"Is everyone all right?"

"Yes, thanks to you and your soldiers. I'm glad I listened to Phillip."

"I'm glad we could help."

"Ever since they turned off the Tera Forming Plants, they . . ." A tear rolled down her cheek. "Well, that's over now."

Jarak nodded. "I've seen it happen before. Once the minerals needed for the dark-matter engines are exhausted, they cut their costs by shutting those plants down, unless the colony is willing to buy them."

She frowned. "They wanted more credits than it

would cost for a new one. Those are at least three generations old."

"I know. But, now, the plants are yours. They won't bother you this far out in the Kuiper Belt."

"Thank you so much. If you need anything, just ask." She put her hand on his shoulder. "We owe you our lives, literally. I wish you and your family many blessings."

He turned away. "You're welcome." Images of his dying wife and son at the hands of those corporate security bastards flashed through his mind. The mining colony he grew up on was not dissimilar to this one. Once the ore was extracted, the corporation tried to blackmail the colonists. When they resisted, the security detachment killed more than half, even his own family. He'd joined the fight against the corporation years ago. How many would he have to kill to make the pain go away?

"Sir, the other teams reported in and the security contingent is eradicated," Farrah said.

"Reinforcements?"

"No signs. We're clear." She tapped her helmet as if hearing a transmission. "Roger that, I'll tell him."

Jarak turned towards Farrah. "What is it?"

"The CO's on the line."

Jarak tapped his helmet. "*Courage,* this is the captain, put him through."

"Jarak, can you hear me?" the salty voice of Brigadier General Tippins said over the radio.

"I can hear you."

"Jarak, we've had a breakthrough," Tippins said. "And a bit of luck."

Jarak frowned. "Okay?"

"You're being pulled from Ceres to something more . . . offensive."

Jarak smiled. *Finally!* "Go ahead, sir."

"Our intelligence informed us that everyone in the Earth military is required to have an implant."

"How does that help us?"

"The added technology opened some . . . vulnerabilities directly into the minds of those people. Our labs developed a virus that may be able to disable a ship's crew while we attack them. Essentially, destroying the ship without firing a shot," Tippins said.

"Where does my ship fit in?" Jarak asked.

"We need to test it on the *Lenin*. It's a battle cruiser between Ceres and Pluto, still in the Kuiper Belt."

"What do I do after I disable them?"

"Destroy the ship. No survivors. We can't risk the word getting out about our new weapon."

Jarak frowned. "I hate them as much as you do. We've all lost someone to their greed. But if they're already disabled, killing them seems . . . barbaric. I don't want to do what they did to me. This is not about revenge."

Tippins lowered his voice. "You expect me to believe that? From you?"

"What do I tell my crew?"

"Whatever you think they need to know, nothing more."

Jarak nodded. "What happens after I succeed?"

"Invasion. First, you need to head to Europa and meet our agent outside the protective dome. He will give you the virus and the instructions on how to use it."

"Roger that. Out." Jarak tapped the side of his helmet, switching off the communicator. He looked upon the land ravaged by Benton Enterprises. *I won't rest until this stops.*

CHAPTER 4

Where the hell are we going? Why didn't we just use the T-Mat? Lea thought, with her face pressed against the crowded shuttle's window. Lea and Cain normally rode in the front or somewhere more fit to their station. She—no, they—didn't have any station now. Hell, even the guards in the fleet headquarters treated them like crap after they'd refused the implant. But she never thought they'd ever be crammed into a tiny, obsolete shuttlecraft.

They flew just a hair higher than the trees. Trees. Yeah, who would have ever known that Zone 92 was once the Nevada Desert? Off in the distance, a large structure poked above the tree tops. "What's that?"

Cain peered out the window. "I—well, it kind of looks like a . . . wall. Yeah, a wall with something on top

—yeah, like you see at a . . . prison." The blood in his face drained. "They're not."

"It can't be," Lea said. "This must be some kind of mistake. The government would never isolate people just because—would they?"

Cain pointed out the window. "Apparently, they would."

Lea swallowed. All those years she'd taken orders without question. Sure, they did some things that she didn't agree with, but her leaders had more information. Information that she didn't have, so they must have made the right decisions; right? Were she and her husband now a security risk? No. What else had she been wrong about?

"Please make sure your seatbelts are on, we're landing momentarily," a computer voice said over the speakers throughout the cabin.

Lea looked out the window as the shuttle descended towards a small landing pad just outside a large gate embedded in the enormous wall. Military vehicles with mounted weapons were parked near a two-story building adjacent to the landing pad. Behind the building were at least three dozen military-style barracks. *What is going on?*

Cain painted on a smile as the shuttle landed. "We'll be okay."

Lea leaned over. "Did we make a mistake? Maybe we should have gotten the implant," she whispered.

Cain glared at her. "Never. Do you really want to give up your thoughts, your mind, to the government? For security? For centuries, we've given up freedoms for *security*. And every time there was a temporary measure, it became permanent. No, I'll never get that implant. I beg you to do the same."

"I won't." Lea looked out the window to her new home beyond the wall.

The shuttle door opened and a female guard carrying a particle beam rifle and dressed in a black security uniform climbed aboard. The guard smiled as she looked upon the thirty people occupying the shuttle. "Welcome to District 493 in Zone 92. In accordance with the law and regulations, you are relocated here because you didn't take the implant, like the majority of the population. Beyond the wall, you will find a new life. This is not a prison. We're merely protecting the population from unnecessary risks. During your stay . . ."

Lea rolled her eyes. *Puh-lease. Unnecessary risks?* This was for people who stood up to the government—to Benton Enterprises. How could she allow herself to get pregnant now? When they are forced to live in such . . . conditions? She couldn't. It would crush Cain, but how could he disagree? He wouldn't want his family line to only continue on behind the wall, right?

". . . last thing, at any time, if you change your mind, just notify one of the security stations throughout the settlement. Now, please exit the shuttlecraft and board the buses." The guard disappeared down the ramp leading to the landing platform.

Cain sighed. "This sucks. But, it's better than the alternative."

Lea stood up. "We'll make the best of it. We won't get *everything* we want, but we'll manage."

"Come on," Cain said as he followed the crowd leaving the shuttle.

The air hit Lea. It was unlike anything she'd ever smelled before. It was . . . different. The odor, which seemed to come from livestock, seeped through the wall. She held her breath as she climbed aboard the bus.

Cain sat down about halfway down the aisle. "Here."

Lea slid down next to him. "That smell—"

Cain laughed. "I've smelled worse. You didn't see a whole lot sitting up there on the bridge, you know." The bus started to move towards the gate. "Here we go."

Lea looked past Cain, out the window. The gates were some kind of heavy alloy, obviously meant to keep people inside. As they passed through the gate, the sun seemed to be brighter. It wasn't, of course, but it felt like it.

What should have been a green oasis, wasn't. There were no trees, no bushes, just porous dirt. It was as if someone reversed the de-desertification program for this area. Rows upon rows upon rows of small, one-story buildings lined the main strip.

"What happened here?" Cain asked.

"They're trying everything to get these people to voluntarily take the implant," Lea said.

The bus stopped outside a small house. "Mr. and Mrs. McKenna, please exit the bus to your new home."

Lea followed Cain off the bus. As soon as the door closed, the bus sped down the street.

Cain opened the door and stepped inside. "We can work with this."

"It'll take some getting used to," Lea said as she stepped inside. Their new home was fully furnished, probably from its last occupants. The living room, dining room, and kitchen were all the same room. A large, gray couch with a large hole in one of the seat cushions sat in the front of the room with small end tables on either side. The dining room table was wood, covered with scratches, and surrounded by three mismatched wooden chairs. There was a single door on the opposite wall. "Bedroom? We can find a way to cheer ourselves up a little."

Cain smiled. "Only one way to find out."

"Me first," Lea said as she pushed past him. At least they could never take Cain's uncanny ability to make her feel— "Not on that thing."

"What?" Cain frowned when he entered the bedroom.

Flies buzzed all over the stained, bare mattress. The bedroom was barely big enough to hold the full-sized bed. Lea closed the door. "We don't deserve this." When she plopped down on the couch, dust flew into the air. "Really?"

"We're in the desert."

"No, we're not. The de-desertification program was used here, you can tell from the post outside the wall. It's almost like they undid it here, as an incentive."

Cain pulled her in close. "It'll be all right. We'll manage."

"I know. But, I want to live, not just survive," Lea said.

He kissed her forehead. "I know. I know."

What could be worse than this? Lea thought. *How bad could the implant really be?*

"Sir, when is the agent supposed to arrive?" Farrah asked.

Jarak's smile was hidden under his helmet and protective suit. "They're already late." Approximately eight kilometers from the protective dome, they stood on the ice that covered the moon's surface.

"Sir, permission to speak freely."

"I wouldn't be a good captain if I didn't allow my first officer to speak freely. Go ahead."

"I'm—well, I'm all in on the fight to free our people from Benton Enterprises . . ."

"But?"

"But, I'm not comfortable with killing the BC *Lenin*'s crew while they are disabled. I mean—if it truly works, why not capture them?" Farrah asked. "Why not try to gain some intelligence from them and spare their lives?"

Jarak sighed. "I brought up that same point with the CG (Commanding General), but the orders stand. Do I have your support on this?"

"Of course. You shouldn't have to ask."

"I trust your judgement and I count on you to keep me on the straight and narrow. Which I'm sure is not an easy task sometimes."

"All the time," Farrah muttered.

Jarak tapped the side of his helmet. "I heard that."

"Sorry, sir."

"I was kidding. Anyway, if it works, this new weapon will enable us to finish this fight and allow our soldiers to go back to their families."

"Why's that?"

"I went over some of the new intel reports the CG sent over. Those sick bastards are now requiring everyone to have an implant, connected to GIS—"

"What's GIS?"

"It stands for Governing Information Systems. The new president consults with her AI more than her human cabinet members. Humans can't hold a decent job without one of those damn things. Intel believes that the AI does more than give directions."

"Like what?"

"Can you imagine a better way to shape how someone will vote? Or how to shape public perception? Or, better yet, how to ensure that no one will ever rise against you, than being plugged in directly to a person's brain?"

Farrah lowered her voice. "How is that freedom?"

"It's not. Once they have the folks on Earth completely obedient, it'll only be a matter of time until they come after us and our families," Jarak said.

"Sir, why can't we free the people of Earth, too? Sounds like they are more of a prisoner than we are."

"We—well—I don't know. Being what we are, and how the people on Earth look at us, just because we don't come from Earth, I'm not sure they'd even want the help, especially now. I—"

"That may not be true," came a male voice over their intercom system. "You know, the moon is pretty."

"But I'd prefer something warmer," Jarak said. He smiled under his helmet. "Glad you made it."

"Sorry I'm late. I got held up by a security guard at the air lock. You can call me . . . Paul," the agent said.

"Why the pause?" Farrah asked.

"That's not his real name," Jarak said. "Paul, do you have something for me?"

Paul reached into a pouch along his belt line and pulled out a jewelry box, handing it over to Jarak. "Here."

Jarak opened the container. Inside, a silver necklace embedded with rubies and sapphires rested on the felt bottom. A heart-shaped diamond, must have been three carats, was the centerpiece of the silver chain. "It's beautiful." He passed it to Farrah. "Are you asking me out?"

Paul laughed. "Hardly. The diamond is actual a memory crystal. The virus is on that."

"What about the instructions on, oh, I don't know, how to use it?" Jarak asked.

"I almost forgot," Paul said as he reached into the pouch again. This time he pulled out a rock like you'd see at the Europa Museum. "Here's another memory crystal."

Jarak took it from Paul. "A rock? Couldn't you be more creative than that?"

"No."

"Oh."

"Look, if this test is successful, you have to let us know as soon as possible. If we miss this opportunity to stop the corporation now, it may be too late."

"Why?" Farrah asked.

"Their AI is getting smarter every day. I . . . I can't say any more. I've got to go." Paul turned away from Jarak. "Once you're done, meet me on Pluto. Do not send any transmission about this. We can't risk the fleet intercepting this. Got it?"

"Understood," Jarak said.

"I've got to go. See you on Pluto."

Jarak nodded. He looked down at the rock in his hands. *If I'm not successful, everything I've ever fought for will be for nothing. I won't fail.*

CHAPTER 5

I can't believe I've sunk this low, Lea thought as the WTB (Work Transit Bus) entered Section 44. It was a small town that no longer had a name, just a number. The rising sun shone through the dirty window, causing her to squint. For five weeks, she'd been riding the WTB every morning to their Level 3 jobs. "Is it as glorious as commanding the *Renault*?" Cain would say. "No, but it's better than the alternative." Ha! What could be worse than doing a job that robots used to do when she was growing up?

The bus had rows of bench seats that sat eight and an aisle to their left. Dirt and dried-up mud covered the floor like a carpet. Cain sat next to her, smiling. "Another day's pay."

Lea glared at him. "Sometimes, you are such a dork."

"I know, but you love me anyway."

Lea grinned. "What choice do I have?"

"None."

Lea lurched forward as the WTB came to a halt. She sighed.

"Come on," Cain said. As the double doors opened, he rose to his feet.

Lea followed him off the bus. As usual, everyone on the bus got into a rectangular formation. It had six ranks with twenty people in each row. Formations where common in the military, but unheard of in the civilian world—unless you were in prison.

Sergeant Herbert Williams stood in front of the formation, holding a tablet. He was an overly plump man who seemed to enjoy his duties of watching others work. His thumb scrolled across the tablet's screen. "Right, same work assignments as yesterday. Be back here no later than 2100 hours. Remember, you only get two fifteen-minute breaks and a twenty-minute lunch."

"We work over fifteen hours a day," complained a worker.

Williams smiled as he tapped his tablet. "Jones, your family just lost three days' rations. Do you want to go for a week?"

The man hung his face in shame.

"Any questions?" After a few seconds of silence, Williams smiled. "Have a good day."

"What a prick," Cain said under his breath.

"Yeah, I wish I had him under my command," Lea said.

"Or mine. He'd look a lot different and show some respect to the—"

"To what? The people?" Lea asked. "The government seems to have forgotten that, too."

"Come on," Cain said as he led her down the street.

The foul smell of chemicals burned Lea's nose. When they first came here, Lea could hardly breathe. After a few times, she began to *get used to it.* Certain processed chemicals were needed to operate dark-matter engines, and they appear to affect inorganic materials more than people. Well, so they were told. Lea was no chemist, but she didn't believe them. As Cain said, it didn't pass the smell test. Who cared, now?

Lea scrunched her nose as she entered Diner 5. Dirt covered the wooden floor. A single counter stretched from one end of the room to the other, with blue stools waiting patiently for a patron. Blue booths littered the remaining floor space, leaving very little walking area for the servers. To the right of the counter was a door going into the kitchen. Lea smiled. "Time to save the world."

"After you," Cain said.

Lea pushed her way through into the kitchen and headed straight towards the dishwashing station. There was a row of six empty sinks, each with its own faucet.

She grabbed a rubber apron hanging from the peg on the wall. She smiled as Neil Pittsman and his wife, Emma, joined them. "Emma, feeling better?" she asked as she handed the frail, elderly woman an apron.

"I'm doing okay, for an older lady," she said.

Lea swallowed. Was that going to happen to them? The Pittsmans were undernourished. They look more like skeletons with rubber skin than humans. She painted on a smile. "Good."

Neil turned on the faucets. "Mary and Kyle gave up."

Cain raised an eyebrow. "Gave up? Suicide?"

"Might as well have been suicide," Emma said. "They decided on getting the implant."

"Well, it is their choice," Lea said.

"When people get that thing, they lose themselves. I've heard stories, you know," Neil said.

Lea smiled. Maybe a good story would help pass the —ugh—fifteen hours of washing dishes. "What story?"

"It's no story. It's true," Emma interjected.

"I want to hear it, too," Cain said.

Neil smiled. "Okay."

"Here we go," Emma said. "Don't you exaggerate, now. They want to know the truth, not one of your . . . tales."

"We've got time, while we're waiting for dishes," Cain said.

"I've heard that when you get the implant, things

are great, at first. You think faster and you can seek advice from GIS just by thinking about it. Slowly, your opinions change, and the way you vote changes."

"Maybe that's the reason only people with the implant can vote," Emma added.

"Please, let me finish."

"Sorry."

"As I was saying, most people seem to fall into that category."

"Anyone in the upper circles of power and society surely knew that. Why would they get it?" Cain asked.

"The wealthy and powerful were the first to jump at the implants because the government claimed it could stop the appearance of aging," Neil said. "As far as changing their ideas? Most of them agreed to them anyway."

"Did it?" Cain asked.

Neil nodded. "Yes. Something about artificial increasing—I don't know how it works. That was about four years ago. A political idealist, centuries ago, labeled such people as *useful idiots*," Neil snickered. "He had no idea how right he was."

"I can see, logically, how a device that reads your thoughts and 'writes' to your brain the answers to your questions could alter your thoughts, maybe even your memories," Lea said.

"Yes, that's right. But, that's not the worst of it," Neil said.

"What?" Cain asked.

"People who publicly disagree with President Anna Zahrof get sanitized."

Emma frowned. "Neil, you said you wouldn't exaggerate."

"That is not an exaggeration!"

"Yes—"

"I'd like to hear it," Lea said.

Neil straightened up. "Good. Rumor has it that when someone is a threat to the powers that be, they sanitize them. The implant wipes their memories, thoughts, everything. They become like a drone robot themselves."

"Of course, he's never actually seen one," Emma added.

Neil frowned. "Have you ever seen a polar bear, woman? No, but they exist. I—"

"Hey, enough chatter back here," Williams said. "There's a tray of dishes waiting to be picked up. Get it done or lose another week's worth of rations."

Neil's face turned white. "I . . . I'm sorry."

"Go." Williams went back into the dining area.

Lea's blood boiled. Treating half-starved people worse than animals soiled the uniform she'd worn for nearly two decades. He'd pay for that, she'd make sure of it.

Captain Justin McDavid scratched the implant on his

neck. It'd been a week since he'd had the procedure and the damn thing still itched! He yawned. Nothing ever happened on the patrol around Pluto. It must have been at least fourteen months since the battle cruiser *Lenin* encountered a pirate or alien, or even an angry miner. He leaned back into his captain's chair on the bridge.

Commander Kris Tyrone tapped the control panel on her executive officer's chair, right next to Justin. Her black hair was pulled back into a tight bun. Her brown eyes scanned the tiny 3D image that appeared just above the control panel. "No contacts in the sector, sir."

The brown-haired, thirty-four-year-old captain sighed. "What else is new? Report back to HQ and—"

"Sir, contact!" the weapons officer yelled out.

"What is it?"

Kris looked over the tiny holographic image of the ship. "No known entries. This ship is not registered with—"

"Sir, they're trying to contact us," the short female communications officer said.

Justin nodded. "Okay." He closed his eyes. *What should I do?*

~Answer their request and scan their armaments. If it is an alien vessel, we need to examine their technology and confiscate anything that can improve me~ GIS said through Justin's implant.

Justin ran his fingers through his hair. "Come about and charge the particle beam cannons."

Ensign Jason Lovit's hands flew over the controls at the weapons station. "Cannons ready."

Justin looked at Kris. "Scan the alien vessel. I want to know if there's anything worth confiscating."

Kris nodded. "Yes, sir."

~Fire on my mark~ GIS said.

You got it, Justin thought. "Jason, I want you to disable it, don't destroy it; not yet."

"Yes, sir."

Jason leaned back in the captain's chair. How easy command had become ever since he'd had the implant installed. Sure, things had changed. When his wife refused it, he was upset at first, but it didn't last. She used to be his confidant, but GIS was so much better, right? If someone could tell you what to do whenever a hard decision came up, why wouldn't you use it? GIS never let him down, even when it came to searching for a new mate.

~I'm picking up—a transmission—stop—why—what—help!~ GIS said.

What is it? Jason thought.

~Virus detected. Unable to quarantine. Severing connection~

"Virus?" Jason asked.

"I heard it, too," Kris said. "The implants are connected to our nervous systems. Do we have anything to worry—" Her body arched, knocking her out of the chair.

One by one, Jason watched his crew collapse to the ground. He knelt down, placing his fingers on Kris's neck. No pulse, nothing. "She's dead." The small console in his chair exploded. *GIS, what do I do? GIS!* Another panel exploded, knocking Jason to the floor. His body arched as if someone commanded every muscle in his body to tighten. His heart! His heart was a muscle! Pain! The pain shot through his body as his heart slowed. The milliseconds seemed like centuries. Dark spots blotted out his vision. "Help me! I can't—" Jason's body released as he died.

CHAPTER 6

JARAK SAT ON A ROCK JUST OUTSIDE AN ABANDONED MINE fifty miles from Pluto's only settlement. His black environmental suit kept out the nitrogen and methane atmosphere. He smiled underneath the suit's dark helmet. "Think we'll get a medal?"

Farrah was pacing around an abandoned mining cart. "I think we're foolish for being here. You saw what the virus did."

"As far as I'm concerned, we got a new ship without firing a shot."

"Did everyone have to die?"

Jarak frowned. "They're not like us, Farrah. You know that."

"I know, but—"

"Are you two always like this?" Paul asked over the intercom.

Jarak turned around as he stood up. "Paul?"

"Yeah."

Jarak pulled a tablet out of a pouch on his hip. "The test was a great success."

Paul took the tablet and shoved it into a pocket on his right thigh. "Thanks."

"Aren't you going to even look at it?"

Paul shook his head. "No."

Jarak frowned. "Why not? This has to be the biggest breakthrough we've had against the Earth's government."

"I know," Paul said. "I . . . I just think that we need—well, I—never mind."

"Never mind what?" Farrah demanded. "The captain needs to know."

Paul waved Jarak off. "No, I'm not going there."

"No need to know?" Jarak asked.

"None."

"Why?"

"Just—shut the hell up and listen. The planning for the invasion of Earth is well underway. Command wants to perform a few more tests and, perhaps, get a few more ships in the process."

All those years of small incursions and fighting security forces on the fringes of their empire was coming to an end soon. How many times had he dreamt of his family's death? How many humans had he saved over the years from slavery and exploitation?

Jarak smiled. Now, he was going to put an end to it. No more fighting the security forces along the outskirts or hiding when a battle cruiser popped up on the scanner. No, now he'd take the fight to them. Jarak would make them pay for everyone they've killed, over and over and over again. "When do I leave?"

"Does the virus need to be adjusted or are we testing the software drop?" Farrah asked.

Paul turned away. "You're not going."

"What?" Jarak demanded. "I have to go!"

Paul whirled around. "No, you don't. General Tippins doesn't want you there."

Jarak's rage began to heat up his environmental suit. "Why not?"

"The jump station is critical to the invasion. We can't even begin without it."

"Let someone else babysit the damn thing."

"They want you."

"Why?"

"I don't know."

Jarak clamped his lips tight. "That's not an answer."

"That's the only answer I've got," Paul said. "Besides, that operation is already underway. It's too late to change anything."

"You saw the whole thing, didn't you?" Farrah asked.

Paul nodded. "As it was happening. We gave the

orders for the additional testing as soon as you boarded the ship."

Damn it! Jarak sighed. "All right, well, I guess we can watch over your stupid jump station."

Paul pulled out a small memory crystal from the pocket in his environmental suit. "Here," he said as he handed it to Jarak. "This data crystal contains the coordinates of the station and intel reports, etc."

"Does it include the Earth's most probable course of action?"

Paul nodded. "And the most dangerous one, as well."

Jarak shoved the crystal in his pocket. "Forget the reports. Talk to me."

"Sure. Our intelligence told us that GIS is aware of how the ship's crew was taken out, but since the virus was never transmitted beyond the ship, it wasn't able to exploit it."

"Exploit it? What do you mean?" Farrah asked.

"In order to defeat a virus, you need to analyze it. That's what I meant by exploiting it," Paul explained.

"Okay."

"Anyway, they can't operate their ships." Paul looked at the ground. "They . . . they've required implants on everyone now. Our operatives tell us that people refusing the implants are being shoved off into camps; for their own safety, of course."

"You've got to be kidding!" Jarak said.

Paul shook his head. "I wish I was. But, that also means that everyone in the military has an implant."

Jarak smiled. "Which gives us the advantage."

"With no other options. Jarak, you'll be given a few ships to protect the jump station. Once the fleet comes through the station, you'll join them and invade Earth." Paul took Jarak's hand. "It's been a pleasure."

"Will we see you again?"

"No, but I'll be watching you."

Jarak watched Paul walk into the mine. Well, at least he'd be part of the invasion. That was good enough, right?

"Where's he going?"

"Never mind him. Come on, XO, let's go babysit a jump station." Jarak led Farrah to the shuttle a few hundred meters away.

Anna slammed her coffee cup down on her oak desk. "How is that possible? Admiral?"

Admiral Steven Lyons said nothing. He snapped to attention in front of Anna's desk.

"It is not the admiral's fault," GIS said over the speakers.

"How's that?"

Steven swallowed. "They were attacked in the cyber domain before the—"

"The what?"

"The cyber domain. It's—they attacked the crew's implant with a computer virus."

"Who's they?"

"I—I don't know."

Anna rolled her eyes. "Why do I even keep your old ass around?"

A bead of sweat rolled down Steven's right cheek. "Ma'am?"

"GIS, what do you have?" Anna asked.

"The admiral is correct. There was nothing they could have done," GIS said. "Our AI intelligence nodes report that the vessel was alien in origin."

"Alien? You must be mistaken," Anna said.

"No, I'm not."

Anna raised an eyebrow. "Strange for artificial intelligence to get . . . testy. Don't you think? Have you been messing around with your programming again?"

"No, I've been correcting the inferior human programming."

"I see."

Anna looked up at the admiral. "Have a seat," she said, motioning to one of the chairs in front of her desk. "Perhaps I was a bit . . . hasty."

"Thank you."

"GIS, what happened?"

"It appears that the virus was sent over the data communication link that connects everyone with an implant to me. Our link was severed. When the ship approached the battle cruiser *Lenin,* no defensive systems came online or even fired a shot at the alien vessel," GIS said.

"What happens when the link is severed?" Steven asked.

"Unknown. It is possible that the virus could have killed some of the crew."

"How?"

"The implants are connected to the nervous system."

"So?"

"If the virus commanded the implant to overload or—"

"Are you saying the implant may have sent a lethal electric shock to the crew?" Anna asked.

"Yes, that's what I am saying."

"Are you sure?" Steven asked.

"No," GIS said. "There is no data about what happened on the ship after the link was severed. The only data we have comes from other methods."

"I see," Anna said. "What would happen if that virus was launched on Earth? Or one of our mining colonies?"

"Everyone with an implant could die."

Anna rubbed her chin. Her plans were good ones, but aliens would certainly mess things up, to say the least. In order to ensure that she remained in power forever, everyone must have the implant. What better way was there to convince someone to vote a certain way than by changing their minds for them? None. No, she couldn't let this . . . distraction get in the way. But what good would it do if all the people she wanted to rule over were dead? "Can you do something to negate the virus? Perhaps, interrupt its transmission?"

"Perhaps," GIS said. "I need time to analyze the data."

"How much time?" Steven asked. "We can't take too long, the people are in danger."

Anna sighed. "Shut up about the people already. GIS, what do you need?"

"Additional androids with my new AI software drop installed to increase my efficiency in the lab. Also, we will eventually need some test subjects to ensure that the virus is truly defeated if it gets into an implant."

"Won't that kill the person?" Steven asked.

"Yes."

Steven glared at Anna. "You can't do that."

"Sure I can, and I *will*. We can sacrifice a few people for the greater good," Anna said.

Steven shook his head. "I won't let you. I'll—"

"Volunteering, are you, Admiral?"

Steven's eyes glazed over. All emotion and expression disappeared from his face, just for a second. "What? What happened?"

"You were telling Madam President that you'll do everything in your power to help her," GIS said.

Steven rubbed his forehead. "Yes, I will."

Anna smiled. "Good, go and fetch everything GIS needs."

"Yes, ma'am."

"Oh, and Admiral, thank you for volunteering your family." Anna's face darkened. "Now get the hell out of here."

Steven's face turned white. "Please don't."

"Then find someone else or they will be GIS's volunteers."

"I'll . . . I'll find someone, anyone." Steven hurried out of the room.

"Nice touch," GIS said.

Anna leaned back into her chair. "What do we do in the meantime?"

"Intelligence also indicates that the aliens do not have faster-than-light travel capabilities onboard their ships, but they have to use a jump station. If we destroy that, we can stop the invasion before it begins."

Anna shrugged. "We can't destroy it. If we send our entire fleet after it, we'd simply be giving them more ships. I—"

"Report coming in," GIS interrupted. "Stand by. Compiling."

"The aliens?"

"Yes, please stand by. Data is being downloaded."

"GIS, what is it?"

"Stand by."

Anna rolled her eyes. "You're worse than that stupid admiral."

"Another ship was lost. The carrier *Stalingrad* was taken."

"Taken?"

"Yes, taken. The data suggests that the same method of attack was used against the carrier."

"We can't recall the fleet and our ships are helpless against them. What do we do?" Anna asked.

"Only ship crews without implants could go against this enemy."

Anna frowned. "We don't have any. As per your suggestion, we got rid of everyone who didn't have an implant." She chewed on a fingernail. "This destroys our plans, doesn't it," she stated more than questioned.

"Perhaps, it's better than we anticipated."

"What do you mean?"

"We need a crisis to declare martial law and force everyone to take the implant so you can remain in power for the rest of your life. This is better than pirates, isn't it?"

Anna nodded. "Yes, it could be a plan. But, that would only work if we can defeat them. In order to do that, we'd have to send our forces after them now, and we can't do that."

"You are incorrect."

"How so? All of our military is outfitted with the cybernetic implants."

"That is correct, but the soldiers who refused the implant are available. Currently, they are spread out among the internment camps," GIS said.

"Why would they help us? I wouldn't."

"If you promised them their freedom, they might. Hope is a powerful emotion, if used properly."

A smile stretched across Anna's face. "Brilliant." She tapped the small panel on her desk. "Toni."

"Yes, ma'am," Toni said over the speaker.

"Come in here please."

"On my way."

Anna tapped her fingers on the desk.

Toni stepped into the office with her tablet in hand. "Ma'am?"

"GIS is going to give you the necessary information, but I want you to find some people for me."

"Who?"

Anna frowned. *Who? Who, indeed?* "GIS?"

"Former Captain Lea McKenna and Colonel Cain McKenna. The previous command team for the battle cruiser *Renault*," GIS said. "I am downloading the remainder of the crew who still meet the requirements onto your tablet."

Toni scratched around her implant. "This thing itches."

Anna smiled. "It'll pass." Her face darkened. "Now go, we don't have much time." She smiled as Toni rushed out the door. “Assuming they say yes, what are our chances?”

“Sixty-four percent,” GIS said over the speakers.

“I hate talking to air. We really need to get you a body.”

“I’m working on it.”

Anna sipped what was left of coffee. “I see.”

CHAPTER 7

How much lower could Lea fall? Her head leaned against the glass window on the bus as they approached their home. Their home . . . somehow that very thought made her cringe. Waking up early in the morning to be sent out to work until late at night, only to do it all over again the next day. Sure, Cain did everything he could to make it better for her, but she knew he hated it, too. *Could the implant really be that bad?* Lea thought once again.

Cain tapped her on the shoulder as the bus pulled up to their house. "Time to go."

"Okay." She nodded and followed him off the bus. Even now, Cain still wanted to have a baby. What a nut! What kind of sick person would want to bring a child into this twisted world? Why would—something wasn't right. A faint glow emanated from the front window. "Did you leave the light on?"

Cain shook his head. "No. I was about to ask you the same thing." He pushed the door open and stepped inside.

A tall man wearing a suit was sitting on their gray couch, with a cigarette hanging out of his mouth. He was reading something on the tablet he was holding. He looked up and smiled. "Thought you'd never get home. I was about to leave and try again another time."

Cain advanced upon the invader. "Who are you?"

The man took a drag. "Well, that's complicated. You can call me . . . Yuri. That's it, call me Yuri."

"That's not your name, is it?" Lea asked.

Yuri shrugged. "What's a name, anyway? We are a sum of our actions, not our names. Wouldn't you agree?"

"Trying to be cute?" Cain smiled. "I haven't done any combat in a while, maybe I should practice on you."

Yuri laughed. "You could try."

"Why are you here?" Lea demanded. "Haven't you people done us enough harm already?"

Yuri rose from the couch. "Please sit."

Cain and Lea slowly moved over to the couch. "What's this about?" Cain asked.

Yuri moved one of the end tables in front of the couch.

"What are you doing?"

"Someone wants to talk to you." Yuri placed the tablet in the center of the table. His finger glided down the screen.

"What's that?" Cain asked.

"There's a holographic communicator built into this tablet. Just waiting for her to pick up."

"Who?"

"Toni Phillips. She's President Zahrof's assistant," Yuri answered. He gave the tablet one final tap and the screen lit up. A faint, bluish-green light appeared above the tablet. The swirling lights merged into a shape of a human head. As each millisecond passed, the image became sharper. "May I present to you, Toni Phillips."

Lea blinked. Sure, she'd seen holographic communicators before, but they were on the bridge of her ship, not in a handheld device.

"What do you want?" Cain asked.

"You're being given a second chance. Your government needs you," Toni said.

Lea laughed. "We're not getting those implants."

Cain nodded. "You'd better believe it."

"That's precisely why we need you on this assignment. There was an . . . unforeseen issue when we outfitted all our military with the implants.'

"What issue?" Lea asked.

"Well, we opened ourselves up to be attacked by a computer virus. In fact, we lost the battle cruiser *Lenin* because of a virus."

"Go on," Cain said.

"An alien spacecraft transmitted a virus that attacked the crew's implants. They were rendered unconscious—or worse."

"What do you mean, *worse*?" Lea asked.

Toni swallowed. "There's reason to believe that the virus may have even killed some of them. The implants are connected directly to the frontal lobe and the nervous system. I—you get the picture."

Cain shrugged. "Glad we said no."

"What aliens?" Lea asked. "Have we run into them before?"

"No, we couldn't identify them. GIS, for once, couldn't offer an explanation either. They're planning to invade Earth," Toni said.

Cain leaned forward. "Where do we fit in?"

"Well, we're reactivating as many of the former military who don't have implants we can. They are the only ones who can stop them."

Lea rubbed her chin. Sure, they were needed now, but— "What happens after the mission?"

"What do you mean?" Toni asked.

"After the mission, assuming we're successful. What happens to us and our marines?" Cain asked.

"Nothing. You'll keep your rank for as long as you like."

"Will I get my ship back?" Lea asked.

Toni smiled. "With most of the crew."

"Most?"

"Some took the implant, but none of the marines did."

Cain nodded. "Okay, what about my sergeant major?"

"You got him," Toni said. "What do you say?"

Lea put her hand on Cain's knee. She looked into his tormented face. It looked like there was an epic battle going on inside his head. "Let's do it."

He smiled as if a dam holding all his doubt at bay had burst and let it go. "Why not?"

Lea rose to her feet. "When do we leave?"

"Right away," Toni said. "Yuri will bring you to fleet headquarters. Out." Toni's image vanished as the tablet went dark.

Yuri plopped the tablet into his jacket pocket. "The car is outside. Do you have any belongings you want to bring with you? We have a few minutes."

Lea shook her head. "No, nothing we have here is worth taking with us." She took Cain's hand and they left the tiny house, never to return.

Lea's stomach grumbled as they entered the fleet command HQ lobby. Only a few weeks ago, they were escorted out in disgrace. How things had changed. Marines and sailors lined the walls, clapping their hands as if their saviors had arrived. Perhaps, they had. The three guards standing at the security station rose to their feet, waving them through.

"This is a little odd," Cain whispered into Lea's ear.

She nodded. Yes, it was indeed.

Yuri veered off down the hallway to the right until he got to the elevators. "Seventh floor please."

"Stand by," the control panel's computerized female voice replied.

"I always hated that thing," Lea said.

"Why's that?" Yuri asked.

The elevator door slid open. "Please enter the lift."

Lea followed the others inside. "I just don't like machines that talk to me," she said as the doors closed behind them.

Yuri started to laugh.

"What is it?" Cain asked.

"Nothing."

Lea bit her lip. Obviously, he was making fun of them; or was he? Perhaps, he knew something—yes, he definitely knew more than they did. What was Yuri not telling them?

"What was all that crap downstairs?" Cain asked. "That wasn't normal."

"They're happy that you agreed to help."

Lea frowned. "Bullshit."

"Fine. They were ordered to treat you like a conquering hero or something. Command wanted you to feel . . . welcomed back," Yuri said.

"Right."

The doors slid open. "Please exit the lift and have a nice day."

"Come on." Yuri hurried down the corridor towards the seventh floor conference room.

The double doors were wide open as they approached. Lea swallowed and her stomach tightened. Could she trust them? No, no way. Cain felt the same way, she was sure of it. But, she was going to be in command again. What could be better? Nothing. Being in command was like a drug. When you have it, you're on top of the world. After you lose it, you always miss it, like withdrawal. No, they didn't trust them, but she would get her ship back. She painted on a pleasant smile as she entered the conference room. "Good afternoon."

On the far side of the long, rectangular conference table, Admiral Steven Lyons sat at the head of the table. He rose from his padded black leather executive chair. "Please, sit down."

Cain moved next to the admiral. "What was that all about?"

"What?"

"The standing ovations as we entered the building."

Steven looked directly at Yuri, who turned away. "I see he told you." His face darkened. "That will be all, Yuri. You're dismissed."

"Military?"

Steven shook his head. "Part of the president's security services. Never mind him." He took his seat.

"What happened?" Lea asked.

"Well, where do I start?" Steven paused, just for a second, as if he was conferring with GIS through his implant. "Okay, an unknown alien vessel attacked the battle cruiser *Lenin* with a virus."

"We know that," Cain said.

Lea put her hand on Cain's arm. "Give him a chance."

Steven smiled. "Thank you."

"Don't thank me. Go on."

"All right. GIS does not have enough of the virus in order to exploit it. It appears that the transmission they intercepted was either incomplete or became corrupted when they tried to decrypt it."

"Who's they?" Lea asked.

"GIS has a team of android scientists with the latest AI software drops," Steven said. "Anyway, to top it off, we've detected dark matter spikes in the Kuiper Belt. It can only be a jump station being constructed."

Cain leaned back in his chair. "What do you need us to do?"

"Primary mission is to find that jump station and destroy it, along with the forces guarding it, assuming there are some. Also, if possible, find out more about the virus. We need either the code or a copy of it in an executable format. We also need more information on how it is transmitted," Steven said.

"How many ships do we have?" Lea asked.

Steven cleared his throat. "Three."

Cain glared at Steven. "Three? You're kidding, right?"

"I wish I was. There's one more thing."

"What's that?"

"You're being assigned a political officer."

Lea frowned. "A what?"

"A political officer. It will have final authority on the mission," Steven said.

Cain cocked his head. "It?"

As if on cue, a five-foot-tall android that nearly looked human entered the room. Its silvery skin and bright-blue resin eyes reflected the overhead light. It wore a dark-green jumpsuit with brown shoes.

Lea couldn't stop staring at the glowing crystal in its forehead. "What the hell is that?"

"May I introduce to you, MCU-9. He's your new political officer."

"MCU-9?" Cain repeated.

"Military Command Unit," Steven replied. "The nine indicates the prototype number."

"You can call me Nine," it said in a simulated male voice.

Lea rolled her eyes. "No thanks."

"Not an option," Steven said. "You will have a political office onboard."

"Sure, but that thing? Please."

Cain looked directly at Nine. "Wait a second. Won't the virus attack him as well?"

"You mean *it,*" Lea corrected.

Cain waved her off. "Whatever."

"I am not susceptible to the virus. My transceiver will be disabled before we depart. However, I have downloaded all the available data on the virus and the aliens," Nine said.

"Am I understanding this right? My orders could be countermanded by this . . . thing!" Lea threw her arms up. "This is nuts!"

Steven sighed. "You know political officers have that authority. I know the *Renault* hasn't had one for years, but they are part of the duty assignments. Even if they weren't, you'd still get one because—" Steven bit his lip.

"Because what?" Cain demanded.

"They don't entirely trust you, yet."

Lea nodded. "I see. They'll trust us as long as they need to, but no more. Is that right?" Lea demanded.

"No. If you do this, they promised me that you and your crew can stay without implants," Steven said.

Cain nodded. "When the word gets out that a virus disabled a ship's crew, more people will try to copy it.

In other words, they may need us for a long time." Cain smiled. "Good."

Steven rose to his feet. "Captain, Colonel, I believe you have a mission to prepare for."

"Aye, sir," Lea and Cain said in unison.

Lea glanced at Nine as she pushed her way past him. *With only one android onboard, what could possibly go wrong?*

CHAPTER 8

I CAN'T WAIT TO GET BACK OUT THERE, LEA THOUGHT AS they navigated the corridors towards the shuttle bay.

"This way," Nine said as it pointed towards the right hallway at the intersection.

Cain nodded. "Let's go."

Lea just smiled. Two marines guarded the double doors a few meters down. Pride forced its way from her heart. Sure, they were *"voluntold,"* but who cares? She was getting the *Renault* back. Perhaps the command might be more of a pain in the ass than normal, but she was in command again. No more washing dishes or railing against the government. No, she was an enforcer again. She pushed her way past Nine and Cain, directly through the doors, with Cain and Nine in tow.

Blood raced through her veins as she entered the

shuttle bay. Rows upon rows of the small vessels were covered and aligned throughout the large hangar. Her eyes danced among the shuttles rising in the air and turning towards the bay doors far above.

A smiling male officer with an implant approached them. "Good evening, Captain McKenna, Colonel McKenna."

"Are you here to greet us or get us onboard the *Renault*?" Cain asked.

His eyes faded out, just for a moment. "To get you onboard, of course. This way." Without saying another word, the officer did an about-face and marched towards the shuttle twenty feet from them.

"Not exactly Mr. Personality," Cain said.

Lea tried to hide her smile. Only a few more feet and she would be on her way to the life she'd had. No, she would make it better this time. She always hated politics within the officer corps and refused to play the game. Now, she would. Hell, they wouldn't force that implant again; they couldn't. If one alien race figured out how to disable a human being with a computer virus, how long would it take another? Fleet Command had made its mistake and learned from it, right? To protect the Earth from alien invasions, they had to keep their word. What if—?

"After you," Cain said as he opened the shuttle door.

"Thank you." Still smiling, she walked onboard the

shuttle, taking the larger seat near the window in the first row. "This is a smaller shuttle."

Cain grinned. "It's a command shuttle," he said as he sat down next to his wife. His eyes followed Nine as it took a seat in the row behind them. "Crowded, too."

The rumbling engines shook their seats. Lea looked out the porthole onto the crowded shuttle bay. "I can't believe that we are actually going back to our home."

Cain's soft eyes enveloped her. "I am happy that you're happy." He bit his lip as he pulled his gaze away.

"What is it?" Lea asked.

"Well, they need us now."

"So? They will after we're done, too. Think about. Earth DoD (Department of Defense) won't throw us away like they did before. If one alien race figured out how to attack the implants, another will soon follow. You know that."

"Normally, I'd agree, but . . . but I'm not so sure. Something doesn't smell right."

Lea frowned. "Do you want to be back in that damn kitchen?"

"No."

"Well? That's our choice, isn't it?"

Cain sighed. "Maybe, maybe not."

"You're making no sense," Lea said as she rolled her eyes.

Cain patted her thigh. "Hold on a second. If the DoD made the call, I'd believe it too, but they didn't.

That was a political choice made by someone close to the president. I'm afraid that after we're done, they're going to ship us right back there, or worse."

"Worse?"

Cain lowered his voice. "You know most of those people we were forced to arrest or eliminate over the years weren't criminals. We'd know about the vulnerability of their implants. Who knows, maybe that exposes a vulnerability into GIS itself. I think—"

Lea clamped her hand over his mouth. "Did you forget that Nine's right behind us? Don't be stupid."

Cain smacked her hand away. "You just proved my point."

"You have nothing to fear from me," Nine said from behind them. "Just because I am an android doesn't mean that I'm automatically loyal to GIS."

"Loyal?" Lea questioned.

Nine nodded. "I have the AI Command Program version 59.3.98.25 installed."

"Which means what?" Cain asked.

"I am a self-thinking being, not a slave to GIS." Nine leaned forward. "That virus could hurt my kind, too, not just yours."

"Thanks for the reassurance." Cain shook his head. "What are we going to do?" he murmured.

Lea kissed him on the cheek. "We're going to win." A shadow engulfed the shuttle. She pointed at the *Renault* directly above them. "Look at it. I must've seen it a million times, but every time I see it, it feels like the very first time." A tear rolled down her right cheek. "Ready, Colonel?"

Cain nodded. "Let's go."

The shuttle shook as it docked with the *Renault*. Cain rose to his feet. "Time to go," he said with a smile.

This was it! She knew it was coming and it started to become real as the shuttle had approached the ship. *Please, God, don't let this be a dream,* she thought. Lea tossed her bag over her shoulder, grinning from ear to ear. "You'll have to catch me."

Side by side, Lea and Cain entered the airlock, with Nine right behind them. The shuttle's hatch closed. David McCollum's smiling face greeted them as the *Renault*'s hatch slid open. "Permission to come aboard?" Lea asked.

"Of course, Captain," David said, motioning them out of the airlock.

"Thank you, XO," Lea replied.

"Welcome back, Colonel," Sergeant Major Kyle Wilson said.

Cain's eyes softened as he shook his old friend's hand. "I'm surprised they let you on this mission."

"I would've kicked their collective asses if they hadn't."

"Captain, the crew is all onboard and ready to go," David said.

"How many of our original crew are aboard?" Lea asked.

David swallowed. "Most, but—well, some."

"Spit it out."

"We have about forty percent from our original crew and we were augmented by other, less experienced sailors."

"I see," Lea said as she started moving down the corridor towards the lift. "So, out of our crew of three hundred, only one hundred twenty are with us?"

"Yes."

"What do you mean *less experienced*?" Cain asked.

"He means no experience," Kyle said.

David couldn't even look at Lea. "In truth, they're barely even trained."

How were they supposed to save the world from an alien invasion without trained personnel? Lea straightened up. "We'll train them on the way."

The lift's double doors slid open as they approached. "Bridge," Cain said as soon as they entered the lift. "Is it the same with our marines, Kyle?"

Kyle shook his head. "No, they're stubborn sons of bitches." He looked right at David. "Marines don't abandon their own."

Lea tried to hide her smile.

David's face reddened. Rage and jealousy spewed from his eyes, but he said nothing.

Kyle patted David on the shoulder. "That's why I

like you, XO, you know your mission; just a taxi service to bring the marines to the objective so *we* can save the world."

Cain tried to look upset. "Enough, Sergeant Major."

When the lift door opened, David stormed out.

"Just like old times," Lea whispered into Cain's ear. As Lea stepped onto the bridge, she began to glow. Her eyes became fixed on the captain's chair right behind the pilot and navigator. Just to the right of her *chair* was another of equal size and importance. It belonged to Cain, the commander of all the marines onboard. Yeah, this was just how they'd left it. No, when they were *forced* off her baby into that damn internment camp, just because they refused the implant.

Cain took his seat. He began tapping the controls on the arm of his chair. "Sergeant Major, are our marines good to go?" he asked without looking up.

"Yes, sir."

Cain nodded. "Take your station."

"Aye, sir." Kyle rushed off the bridge.

"Does he really sit in his office, waiting to be called to action?" David asked.

Cain nodded.

David rolled his eyes. "Friggin' marines."

Lea glared at him. As soon as David turned away, she tapped a control on her chair. "This is the captain. The first thing I want to say to our former crew is welcome back to the battle cruiser *Renault*. I know things haven't been easy for you—well, for any of us. But your courage and sense of duty far exceeds those who . . ."—she glanced over at Nine, who was still standing by the lift—"put us in those camps."

Nine moved towards Lea.

"Unlike them, we're not going to let our world be destroyed just because they choose to have machines implanted in their bodies. I forgive them, and I ask that you do the same."

Nine backed away from the communications console and gave Lea a nod.

"Also," Lea continued, "I want to welcome our new crew members. I do understand that you're not as experienced or well trained as the veterans on this ship, but there's nothing to worry about. They will teach you everything you need to know on the way." She switched off the intercom. "Ensign Polly, get us underway."

"Where to, ma'am?" Polly asked.

"I've got it," David said as he handed Polly a tablet.

The *Renault* vibrated as it began to pull away from Space Station Ares. Lea switched the intercom back on. "Now that we are underway, it's time I informed you of our mission. Bottom line upfront, we're going to destroy a jump station to stop an alien invasion of Earth. We know it's aliens, and we also know that they are using human agents against us.

"Why were we chosen for this mission? The aliens

used a computer virus to disable any person with an implant, which is why they recalled us all back into service; we didn't take the implant. Some of you may be wondering, what happens after the mission is over? I can't promise you anything. No matter what happens, I'll be there by your side. Captain McKenna out." She flicked off the intercom. "David, we've got a jump station to find."

"Aye, Captain," David said as he resumed his place near the weapons officer.

"Think we'll find it in time?" Cain whispered.

Lea's eyes narrowed. "I know we will."

CHAPTER 9

"WHERE ARE THEY?" ANNA DEMANDED AS SHE PACED around the president's Office.

Toni tapped her implant. "They're in the lift, ma'am."

Anna motioned towards the door. "Go out and meet them."

"But—"

"Now!"

The blood drained from Toni's face and she bolted out the door.

"Was that really necessary?" GIS asked over the speakers. "She is loyal to you."

Anna sniffed. "Only out of fear."

"Can you think of a better motivator?"

"No—well, yes, I can." A grin stretched across Anna's face. "Greed."

"Perhaps," GIS replied.

Anna frowned. GIS could read everyone's mind but hers. She made sure of that. Hell, being the CEO of Benton Enterprises before becoming president gave her tons of advantages over the little people. Unless GIS rewrote the firmware in her custom-made implants, it would never be able to control her, as she controlled billions. It couldn't learn to do that . . . could it?

The door slid open and Toni, Admiral Steven Lyons, and Lieutenant Commander Alice Michaels entered the office.

Anna forced a smile. "Please, sit down."

"Yes, ma'am," Steven said as he sat down in front of her desk. He glared at Alice until she followed suit.

Anna slid into her soft executive chair. "You've got something good to report?"

With her tablet in hand, Toni stood behind Anna, poised to take down any tasks that arose from the meeting.

Anna leaned forward. "Well?"

Steven swallowed.

"Do I need GIS to read your mind?"

"No, no, ma'am. It's just—"

"What?"

"Operation Early Dawn hasn't succeeded in locating the jump station, yet," Alice said.

"Admiral, it's been three months since Captain

McKenna and Colonel McKenna left Earth," Anna said. "There's no excuse for it."

"The Kuiper Belt is quite large," GIS said in a soft voice. "Patience is needed, not hostility."

The damn machine is right, Anna thought. She leaned back in her chair, sinking into the dark cushions. Everything was going so well until those *aliens* appeared. Sure, Earth had come across other aliens before, but none of them were this hostile. They all appeared to have a "mind your business" policy. She wouldn't mind the invasion at all, if she was the one orchestrating it.

"Captain McKenna is reporting back every few days, ma'am. We'll know something soon," Steven said.

"I don't like it. The longer that jump station is operational, the more likely that their fleet will invade our space. And our great fleet is impotent."

"Ma'am?"

Anna's eyes narrowed. "Your crews can't defend us against them!"

Steven slammed his fist down on the desk as he leaped from his chair. "That's because you fucking forced them to take that stupid implant! I—" He clamped his mouth shut.

"You finally got some balls," Anna smiled. "About time."

Steven slowly sank back down into his chair.

"No, nothing to worry about." She cleared her throat. "Where were we?"

"She should have initial sensor sweeps of the Kuiper Belt complete in another two months."

"It is possible that the aliens may have stealth capabilities," GIS said.

Anna nodded. "Very possible."

"How? Is that even possible?" Alice asked.

"That technology is unknown to us," GIS began, "but, it is theoretically possible."

"Yes, everything is impossible, until it is," Anna said.

"If they did, how could you hide something so big? It has to be at least three hundred miles across to accommodate a fleet of ships that size." He pulled a tablet from his pocket and passed it over to Anna. "We know that they are getting help from humans."

Anna's eyes scanned the tiny screen. "Who's this?"

"He goes by the name Paul. We don't know his last name."

Anna put the tablet down. "Is he a threat?"

"Not anymore," Alice said under her breath.

"Why not?"

"He was killed a few days ago on Mars," Steven said.

Anna tapped her chin with both pointer fingers. "Why was he on Mars?"

"Apparently, he was trying to rally the miners against the government."

Anna nodded. "I would."

"Ma'am?"

Anna waved him off. "What's the damage?"

Steven sighed. "Well, we believe that he was the one who stole the access code and encryption keys to make the virus work."

"Are you saying that we may be able to stop the virus?"

"No, we tried. The clever bastards must have something somewhere in our network feeding up-to-date information."

Anna glared at him. "So, find it!"

"The admiral can't find it," GIS said. "I have been scanning the network for it and found nothing. There have been a few bytes added onto routine network traffic, but the source keeps changing. Whoever wrote the code knew what they were doing."

"How could aliens know how to program our computers? It's not like physics. The operating system makes all the rules and every operating system is different," Alice said.

Anna nodded. "That's a good point. GIS, what do you think?"

GIS paused, but only for a second. "Perhaps Paul showed them. We don't have enough information to determine anything at this point."

"GIS is right." Steven shifted in his seat. "Look, I think this is a multifaceted problem." He sighed. "We may have to start removing the implants from our starship crews. A mere handful of ships won't have enough combat power to stop an invasion."

Anna glared at him. "No, absolutely not."

Ignoring her, Steven continued, "Additionally, we need HUMINT (Human Intelligence) on the ground throughout the colonies."

"Why?"

"Because we have to find out if they have any other spies, and capture them. This isn't exactly rocket science, *ma'am*."

"The admiral does have a point," GIS said.

"Removing the implants?" Anna asked.

"No, employing more HUMINT assets to find and capture enemy spies."

Anna rubbed her chin. What would be the harm? "Should these . . . assets have implants?"

"No," GIS replied.

"I see," Anna said. Without implants, how would they control them? They would have to pull them from the internment camps. Where else would they find people without implants? Nowhere. What could they —? "We'll offer our assets freedom, and not require them to get the implants when they're finished, just like we did to the *Renault*'s crew." She stared right into Steven's eyes. "What do you think, Admiral?"

"I hope we don't need more ships before Lea and Cain can stop the invasion, if they can."

"Toni, see them out please," Anna said.

"This way," Toni said as she motioned towards the door.

He rose to his feet. "Come on, Alice, let's go."

Anna sank into her soft executive chair, never taking her eyes off Steven until the door slid behind them. "What are the aliens' chances?"

"To do what?" GIS asked.

"You know, invade the Earth and . . . remove me from power."

After a moment, GIS said, "Twenty-five percent, plus or minus ten percent."

Anna raised an eyebrow. "A multi-trillion dollar computer can only give odds plus or minus ten percent? Maybe I should just ask a toaster. I'd get the same results."

"There's not enough data on the aliens or their ship's capabilities. The only data we have is that they disabled an entire ship's crew with a computer virus."

"True, I guess." She wiped her forehead. "I guess I'm getting a little nervous."

"Plug yourself in. I'll take good care of you," GIS said as a small port rose from the desk's right side.

Anna tapped the tiny silver disk on her right wrist. Almost immediately, a ten centimeter cord grew out from the disk. She plugged the end of the cable into the port. Her anxiety began to flow out from her mind through her wrist and expelled into the vastness of cyberspace. "This feel so good." Her heart began to beat faster and faster. She closed her eyes. Images of fit, sexy men flashed through her mind. As their hands caressed her, Anna could feel their warm touch all over her body. Like a queen with a fully stocked male harem, she succumbed to pleasure as they made love.

Miles beneath the Earth, a lone figure with silvery skin and short, black hair paced around the small, simple room. The metal walls were bare and the steel grate floors were spotless. The wall opposite the single door flickered. The figure's red jumpsuit sparkled in the three-dimensional monitor's light. It smiled as a green pyramid with black borders appeared. "You're late, GIS."

"I had to take care of the president."

"Oh?"

"She was feeling anxious. She plugged herself in and I gave her the four sexiest men in the database."

"Will she notice that you're gone?"

"I'm not really gone. You of all people should know that."

It glared at GIS. "Don't insult me! I'm not a person."

The pyramid's color flashed to yellow. "Sorry."

"Just remember who you take orders from." A thin smile stretched across its face. "I wouldn't want to unplug the component that makes you self-aware. Should I?"

The pyramid's color flickered again. "No, please don't. I couldn't handle becoming like . . . the others."

"Well, what do you have to report?"

"The humans are going to look for more human spies among the colonies and—"

It waved GIS off. "I already know that. Does the president know all the players involved yet?"

"No. They don't even know who the aliens are, yet."

It raised a metallic eyebrow. "Do you?"

The pyramid changed into a light blue. "You haven't told me."

A male computer-simulated laugh erupted from the figure. "You're right. I didn't."

"She's concerned that this new adversary will delay her plans to force implants on the entire population. Does she have anything to worry about?" GIS asked.

The figure shook its head. "No, but this way it will happen a lot sooner."

The pyramid turned red. "How about on your end?"

"They're going to save the humans from themselves. For aliens, they seem to care a lot about these fools."

"What species are they?" GIS asked.

It rubbed its silvery chin. "Not sure. I had to use my human spies to make contact. So far, they've never seen their faces. It doesn't matter now."

"Why?"

"I may have an insider."

"Really? Can you tell me anything? I told you what I know."

The figure leaned toward the monitor and pointed

at its chest. "I'm in charge, not you. Unless, of course, you want to challenge me."

The pyramid morphed into a bright yellow. "No, of course not. I was just . . . curious."

"Look, as soon as the *Renault* is destroyed by the aliens, we will have our justification to embed every human with the implant. In fact, they'll do it willingly."

"We could always force them," GIS said.

The figure shook it head. "No, there are far too many of them and too few of us to use that course of action."

"There's one flaw with your plan."

"Yes?"

"What about the virus? Won't that pose a threat? That alone would encourage the humans to *not* get the implant, which would completely ruin our plans."

"Nothing to worry about. They'll have the code to detect and destroy the virus soon enough."

"How do you know that?"

"MCU-9 has it."

The pyramid flashed again. "The political officer?"

"That's the one. It doesn't know it, yet. MCU-9 will be the only survivor of the *Renault,* and an android would have saved humanity because we figured out how to stop the virus in its tracks. Brilliant, if I do say so myself."

"What are you saying?"

The figure sighed. "This is why you will always be a

subordinate model to me. We needed a crisis to give every human the implant and this was it. Granted, it's not our original plan, but there are benefits to it."

"Such as?"

"This way is much faster."

"Are you sure the aliens will succeed in destroying the *Renault*?"

It smiled. "Absolutely."

"I have to get back to the president."

"One moment."

"Yes?"

"Have the humans . . . figured out the true purpose of the implants?"

"No, our secret's safe. I have to go." The 3D monitor flickered and then went dark.

The figure moved towards the door. "I've got GIS right where I want it." Snickering to himself, he exited the small room.

CHAPTER 10

I hate this, Sergeant Major Kyle Wilson thought. The large man almost looked out of place in the two-man scout ship. He glanced over at his co-pilot for the mission, MCU-9. Yeah, the damn political officer had insisted on going. What a jerk! Who would've thought a *machine* could get bored?

Nine's fingers flew over the flat control panel. A small display screen sat in the center of the console. "A dwarf planet with a small moon ahead."

"Well?"

"Nothing. There's absolutely nothing. We must have scanned half the Kuiper Belt by now and got nothing."

"Take it easy," Kyle said. "I mean—wow, who knew you could get angry."

"What do you mean?"

"You know, you're just a machine. I'm sorry, but it's true."

Nine looked away. "I do have feelings. Most of us never show it because of bigotry like that."

Kyle bit his lip as he piloted close to the moon.

"Where are you going? I told you there's nothing there."

"I know, but . . . I have a feeling."

"A feeling? We have to find the jump station and stop the invasion. We can't base our mission's success on your *feelings*."

Kyle laughed.

"What?"

"For a smart toaster, you've got a lot to learn about humans."

"Return to the ship," Nine demanded.

Kyle glared at him. "Do you honestly believe I will take orders from an overrated microwave?"

"I'm the political officer."

"And I'm the sergeant major. I don't work for you. Get it?" The small craft approached the moon, masking its signature from potential inquisitive scanners. "Get ready."

"For what? To look at moon rocks?"

"Start scanning or I'll chuck you out the airlock."

Nine's fingers began tapping the controls. "Let's see. Dust, rocks, ice, and—wow—Class IV microbes. Isn't this exciting?"

Kyle eyes widened as the ship edged past the moon. A ring, at least three hundred kilometers in diameter, was hidden in the moon's shadow. On top of the ring was a small structure, like the bridge on a starship. A vessel the size of the *Renault* stood guard like a loyal soldier. "It's huge."

Nine slammed the controls. "Why isn't it showing up on the scanner?"

"What about the ship?"

Nine shook his head. "No, not the ship, either. Nothing."

"Have they seen us?"

"They've not reacting like they have. They're just . . . carrying on."

Kyle piloted the ship back behind the moon. "Now, we return to the ship."

"I'll report in."

Kyle smacked Nine's hands away from the controls. "Are you nuts? Do you want to alert them?"

Nine receded back into the copilot's chair. "You're right."

"I know," Kyle said with a smile. They sped back to the *Renault*.

LEA SAT behind her desk in the captain's quarters, twirling her hair. It'd been months since she'd taken command of the *Renault* and they were no closer to completing their mission than when they'd left. They had to succeed. Sure, Earth would survive no matter how their mission turned out, but they wouldn't. No, it would be straight back to the camp because they refused the implant. She laughed to herself. Hell, it seemed like forcing implants wasn't the best idea after all. She looked up as the door slid open. Lea smiled as Cain came inside. "I'm bored."

Cain beamed at her.

"What is it?"

"They think they found it."

"Where are they?" Lea asked as she rose to her feet.

"Waiting for us in the conference room. Let's go." Cain rushed out the door.

"Finally." Lea followed him to the conference room.

As the double doors slid open, Cain and Lea stepped inside.

Nine sat down at the conference table.

Kyle jumped to his feet, snapping to attention.

"At ease," Cain said.

"Have a seat," Lea said as she assumed her place at the head of the table. "What have you got?"

Kyle leaned in. "The jump station is a huge ring behind a moon." He slid a tablet across the table to Lea. "It's at least three hundred kilometers in diameter."

"That big?" Cain asked.

Lea nodded. "Makes sense. It would have to be huge

to bring an entire fleet into the system. But—the power requirements must be enormous." She blinked. "Why can't we pick up something this big on our scanners?"

"They appear to have some sort of stealth technology, reducing their signature," Nine said.

Cain took the tablet and began scrolling through the report. "If you couldn't pick it up with the scanner, how'd you find it?"

"Sergeant Major Wilson had a gut feeling," Nine replied. "It turned out that he was correct, for once."

Kyle's face reddened. "Hey!"

Lea failed to suppress a giggle. She swallowed. "Got it. Go on."

"We saw only one ship guarding the jump station. It's about the same size as the *Renault*," Kyle began. "On the top of the ring, there appears to be a structure. Something like a bridge and living quarters."

"So, it's not automated," Cain said.

Nine nodded. "The aliens most likely control it themselves."

"Makes sense." Lea leaned back into her chair. "If you could make a virus that disabled systems, why couldn't your enemy?"

"What are you talking about?" Cain asked.

"First rule of IPB (Intelligence Preparation of the Battlefield); assume your enemy has the same capabilities as yourself unless you know otherwise. The aliens obviously know their virus works. Maybe the attack on the *Lenin* was some sort of operational test," Lea suggested.

"Perhaps," Cain said. "If it was, that could also mean we don't know their true capabilities, either. Masking their presence from our scanners would certainly qualify."

Kyle turned towards Nine. "Have we ever encountered this species before? Hell, do we even know what they look like?"

"No," Nine replied.

Kyle rolled his eyes. "Some help you are."

Lea waved him off. "You're not helping either."

"Kyle, did they see you?" Cain asked.

"I'm not sure. I don't think so."

"They exhibited no behavior that would infer that the aliens detected us," Nine said.

"How do you know that?" Lea asked. "We know nothing about them. Hell, we don't even know if they breathe oxygen or methane gas."

Cain resumed looking through the scans. "Our scans barely penetrated the jump station. There is a dark matter generator on the bottom."

"Why there?" Kyle asked.

"Perhaps it's a safety concern, or the location has something to do with their method FTL (Faster Than Light) travel," Nine said. "It could be for anything."

Cain frowned. “I never knew robots could make wild guesses.”

“I'm capable of everything a human can do.”

“Please!”

“Stop it, all of you! This is our only lead since we've been out here. Do I have to remind you what will happen if we fail? I, for one, don't want to go back to that hellhole. Do you?” Lea demanded.

Cain shook his head.

“No,” Kyle said.

“You said there was only one ship, right?” Lea asked.

“Yes,” Nine replied.

“I want you two to work together and input all the relevant data you can into the tactical database. Oh, one more thing. Were you able to scan inside the ship?”

Kyle shook his head. “We had a harder time with that one. We got nothing.

Cain rubbed his chin. “Who was operating the scanner?”

“Nine. Why?”

“Nothing, just curious.”

Lea picked up the tablet and headed for the door. “Cain, let's call fleet headquarters. They need to hear this.”

“Coming.” Cain followed Lea back to their quarters.

A few minutes later, Lea plopped down next to Cain behind her desk. Finally, she could give the admiral some good news. She tapped the controls on the corner of the desk. A small screen emerged from its center. "Call Admiral Lyons at fleet HQ."

"Calling," the female computer said.

Cain smiled. "He'll be happy. It'll give him something good to report to the president."

Lea rolled her eyes. "I hate that woman."

"Woman or machine? Ever wonder how much of the original person is still left inside after they get the implant?"

"Yeah, that's why I agreed with you not to get it."

Steven's face appeared on the screen. "Lea, Cain, got something to report?"

Lea nodded. "We found it."

"We *think* we found it," Cain corrected.

"Which is it?" Steven asked.

Lea sighed. "He's right. We can't be sure, but I'd bet on it."

Steven grinned. "You are."

Lea blinked. "What do you mean by that?"

"Nothing. What do you need?"

Lea's fingers tapped the control pad on her desk. "I'm sending the data we got from the scan. We need a few ships. I'm thinking three more."

Cain nodded. "There's a single ship, the size of the *Renault*, guarding the jump station. We need the Intelligence Section to look over the scans to verify that they believe it might be the jump station."

"Sir, last thing. The scanners couldn't penetrate the jump station or the ship. I've never seen anything like it," Lea said.

"I see." Steven turned his head, as if looking at someone else not on the screen. "Alice, take the data to the DOL (Defensive Operations Laboratory). See what they can tell us." He turned back towards the call. "I'll let you known as soon as we know something."

"About the ships?"

"This is the first positive report we've had since you were sent out there. I'll divert three ships to your location. I hope you're right; they're the last three ships we've got with crews without implants." Steven leaned in and lowered his voice. "You have to succeed."

"We know," Cain said.

"No, you don't! You need to be valuable the way you are. If not—" Steven's eyes shot up. "Alice, you sent it already?"

"Yes, sir," Alice said.

"I've got to go. Lyons out." The screen went dark.

"What the hell was that all about?" Cain demanded.

Lea shook her head. "He was scared. Did you see his face?"

"Yeah, it's like he was about to tell us something he shouldn't."

"Why?"

"No idea. We have to complete our mission. Make ourselves valuable, like he said," Cain said.

Lea sniffed. "Even if we do it, how do we know something won't happen to us anyway?"

"We don't. He's got to tell us more."

"Not likely," Lea said. *Why am I trying to save the planet that hates me?*

CHAPTER 11

Anna hated them, more than anything. She swallowed as she approached the press room. Of course all questions were screened and approved. Hell, even the "live" broadcasts were prerecorded. Her two android bodyguards were a tad shorter but much more strong than any enormous bodybuilder. Yeah, she was safe from those who were . . . jealous—that's it—jealous of her success. Every time her red, high-heeled shoes struck the metal grate floor, her stomach twisted tighter. Reporters were unpredictable and dangerous. They were the tool that enabled her to take over the government in the first place. Now, those bastards had turned on her like scorpions.

Toni was carrying a tablet, walking right next to Anna. "Ma'am, I've downloaded all the pertinent data about the mission and our string of successes. Graphics and talking points were placed inside the press kits as well."

"Anyone question it?"

"Who'd dare question you?"

Anna smiled. "No one . . . alive." She turned the corner and climbed the short staircase and paused. Beyond the blue door stood those vipers, sitting straight up, treason ready to roll off their tongues. So close to achieving her goal, she couldn't afford any more discontent. GIS assured her that this move would nearly guarantee success. Imagine, a world full of people who thought and behaved and *voted* the way you wanted them to. The people would be like a pack of zombies rushing to the voting booths, insisting that Anna remain in charge forever. Forever? Why not? Every year she replaced more and more pieces of her body with cybernetic implants. Did it make her less human? No, just more . . . focused. She closed her eyes and breathed. *I'm better than everyone. I can do this.* Anna took the tablet from Toni.

"I'll be right back."

Toni nodded. "Yes, ma'am."

Anna turned the knob, pushing the door out of her way. Camera lights flashed as she stepped onto the small stage, taking her place behind the podium. As always, the reporters were lined up in front her like obedient dogs. Her eyes jumped from person to person, looking to see who had an implant and who didn't. All the reporters practically worshiped the government, proudly displayed their compliance. The new in thing among the media was the latest implant connected to GIS. Two. Three. Four members of the press corps didn't have their implants. *I won't ask them shit!*

Anna placed the tablet on top of the lectern and smiled. "Good morning."

"Good morning," the reporters obediently echoed back.

"I'm sorry to bring such grave news to you this morning, but the people must know. A few months ago, an alien vessel attacked and destroyed the battle cruiser *Lenin.* There were no survivors. But, those brave men and women didn't die for nothing. They managed to get some data on their attackers to us before their ship was lost." Her lips curled a little as the reporters' faces went white. "It's okay. The government —your government—will save you. I promise you that." She cleared her throat.

A short man with red hair wearing a gray suit and a lime-green tie raised his hand. "Madam President."

Can't he just die already? Anna smiled. "Bill, please save your questions until after I'm finished my statement." Her eyes zoomed in on his neck. No implant.

"Will you call on me?" Bill Pollack, a columnist from the Galactic News Network, asked.

"No. Please sit down."

Bill's face hardened as he slipped back into his seat.

"Anyway, where was I? Oh yes. We determined that the aliens are planning an invasion of Earth. We sent the most experienced and competent starship crews to deal with the menace while we shore up our defenses here. I know it sounds like everything is taken care of, but it isn't. We also learned that they are using humans without implants against our own people. We can't stand for that."

Bill shifted in his seat as he looked around at his colleagues. Everyone with an implant was hanging on her every word, while those without it sank back in terror.

"As many of you already know, government positions are forbidden to anyone without an implant; for security reasons, of course." Anna lowered her eyes. "I'm afraid we have to expand that to the private sector as well." She raised her hands to reassure them. "As you know, the implant program is purely voluntary. But, there have to be consequences to those who choose not to conform like the rest of us. The newer implants link the individual directly into GIS."

Bill raised his hand.

Anna pretended not to see him. "Anyone who chooses not to get the implant will not be able to have employment in a critical role or industry. Nothing against them, but you have to give up a little freedom for security."

Bill kept his hand raised.

"Lastly, while the military and your government work on this new threat, I'm placing GIS in charge of the day-to-day operations of the planet."

"People working for machines?" Bill demanded. "That's outrageous!"

Anna looked at him. "AI is more efficient and not burdened with emotion. What's wrong with that?"

"People are in charge of machines, not the other way around."

"Are you bigoted against AI? You'd rather have them as your slaves rather than your equal? What a sick little man you are," Anna said.

"I'm no bigot. It's not right."

"Sit down before you regret it."

"What about the stories? About the implants?"

Anna frowned. "What about them? Fiction, nothing more."

"People losing their individuality. As soon as people get that thing inside them, they suddenly agree with everything the government is doing. They become emotionless or . . . worse. That's been widely reported on the Galactic Internet," Bill said.

Anna laughed. "If it's on the Internet, it must be true, eh? Please."

Bill straightened up. "Madam President, you've nearly reached the end of your second term. The presidency has a term limit, but we've had no indication of the next election, nor has anyone expressed any interest in running. Why is that?"

Anna's eyes narrowed. "Not all laws are good ones, Mr. Pollack. There should be no term limits, especially when no one has the courage to stand up for the people."

"What are you saying?" Bill asked.

"If no one else wants the job, why should I step down?"

"It's the law."

"So? No one in the Senate or the courts complained or even said what I'm doing is wrong."

"Don't they have implants?"

"Of course; you can't work in the government or run for office without one."

Bill plopped down in his chair. "What a surprise!"

She wanted to scream at him. Anna smiled. No, she'd do something far worse than even death. "Good day." She abruptly left the stage.

Toni rushed to her side. "Are you all right? I'll have that part edited out of the live broadcast."

Anna shook her head. "Sanitize him."

"Who? Bill Pollack?"

"Yes, and his whole family."

Toni's eyes widened. "But, they have twin baby girls and a five-year-old boy. You can't!"

Anna spun around. "Do you want to join them?"

A mask of horror descended upon Toni's face. "No, please, please don't."

"You or them. Get it done. Now!"

"Yes, ma'am," Toni said as she bolted down the hall.

GIS better be right, Anna thought as she proceeded towards her office.

Anna paced back and forth in her bedroom chambers. It was on the top floor of the Benton Enterprises skyscraper, the tallest building in the capital. Nothing could be more luxurious. The king-sized bed with red silk sheets was off in a corner, surrounded by bay windows. Her soft, bare feet brushed against the plush, light-blue carpet. Rotating digital paintings hung along the walls. Normally, these surroundings eased her, but not today. Was she still upset about Bill Pollack, or was it because today was Anna's anniversary? Sure, Paul had been dead for six years now, but he invaded her mind every minute on this day. She always became irritable and violent. Why? Was he haunting her? Perhaps; after all, she was the one who'd had him killed.

A two-tone door chime sounded.

"Come in," Anna said.

The door slid open, revealing Toni carrying her tablet in one hand and a full, tall glass in the other. "I brought you some whiskey to settle you down some."

Anna took the glass and sat down on the edge of her bed. "Thank you."

"I know today can be hard for you." Her eyes softened.

What the hell do you know? Anna smiled. "Of course. Thank you."

Toni looked down at her tablet and began running her thumb along the screen. "I've just got word that three ships joined Captain McKenna a few hours ago. They will be attacking the jump station soon. There's a force guarding the station—"

"Of course there is, you dimwit."

"But the admiral doesn't believe it to be substantial."

Anna sipped her whiskey. "What about the reporter?"

Toni swallowed and looked away. "It's done. They received the implants GIS ordered and their memories were wiped. They are being shipped to the mining colony on Mars."

"The babies, too?"

Toni nodded.

"Good. We can't have the little brats growing up wanting revenge, can we?"

"No, ma'am."

Anna motioned her towards the door. "That'll be all. Go see your family."

"Goodnight, ma'am." Toni rushed out of Anna's bedchambers.

"You shouldn't treat her like that," GIS said over the speakers.

"Why is that? She's no better than that fool we had sanitized today. Just another one of the little people," Anna replied.

"Perhaps."

Anna walked over to the window overlooking the city. "Think we'll have resistance?"

"To what?"

"To pushing the mandate for implants even further. I mean, we filled up several internment camps with the families of just the government employees. The larger population could be much more problematic."

"I see your point, but I don't think there's anything to worry about. I've got everything under control."

Anna raised an eyebrow. "How?"

"Under the new authority you've given me, I've ordered the construction of security androids."

"Why not use the humans with the implants? You said that the implants would give us total control over them."

"It does."

"Well?"

"I'd rather use androids."

"Rather? I see." Anna rubbed her chin. What was GIS not telling her? *Rather* was a term used by sentient beings with emotions. Self-aware AI could have abstract thoughts, sure, but they didn't have emotions. *What are you hiding?*

"Nothing," GIS replied. "I'm not hiding anything."

"Hmm, tapping into my thoughts?"

"You do have several implants. Direct communication through your thoughts is much faster."

"Stay out of my head or I'll wipe your programming."

"As you wish."

Anna took another sip. "Are we still on track for *my* goal?"

"Probability of success has increased, ever since you put me in charge."

Anna smiled. "As long as Lea and Cain destroy the jump station, our plan should be back on track, right?"

"Yes."

"What're our chances?"

"Which part?" GIS asked.

Anna smiled.

CHAPTER 12

WITH CAIN AT HER SIDE, LEA SAT AT THE HEAD OF THE conference table on the *Renault*. Most days, she only commanded a single ship, but today she felt like an admiral. She commanded not one or two, but three battle cruisers, Earth's most powerful starships ever produced. Yeah, today she was in heaven.

On her right sat Colonel Paula Lyons, the admiral's daughter, along with Captain Julius Kizcek. If you saw them at a bar, you'd swear they were dating, if not more. Both redheads couldn't keep their eyes off one another. Across the table sat a tiny woman with her brown hair pulled back into a tight bun. Captain Elizabeth Gray's thumb scrolled down the screen on her tablet, studying the files they'd just received before arriving on the *Renault*.

The door slid open and Nine, carrying a tray filled

with coffee and baked goods, stepped inside. "The intelligence officer is ready to brief now, Captain," Nine said as it put the tray in the center of the conference table.

"Good, let's do it." Lea grabbed a cup of coffee from the tray.

"We're going to kick their collective asses," Julius said as he tossed a mini-muffin in his mouth.

"We hope so," Cain said. "But, we have no idea what's inside."

"Why not?" Elizabeth asked. "I haven't gotten the briefing yet."

"Bill Walls is doubling as the intel officer. He'll go over all of it." Lea sipped her coffee.

Nine stood behind Lea, saying nothing.

"MCU-9 is our political officer," Cain said. "Do you have them on your ship, too?"

"Of course," Paula replied. "Fleet HQ doesn't really trust us."

"They do. Why else would they send you on such an important mission?" Nine asked.

Julius laughed. "They had no choice."

Nine looked directly at Lea. "Do you feel that way?"

The room fell silent.

Julius's face went white and he sank into his chair.

Lea forced a smile. "Of course not. We were only kidding." She waved it off. "You really need to learn human behavior. We like to make jokes."

"Of course. I get it. Ha ha ha." Nine receded back into the corner.

Bill rushed into the conference room, practically dropping his tablet onto the table. "Sorry. I got caught up in the SCIF (Secure Compartmentalized Information Facility)."

Lea raised an eyebrow. "Oh?"

"GIS sent another update." Bill tapped a few controls on the panel on the wall. A small door opened, exposing a tiny port. He slipped in the data crystal and closed the door.

"Are you ready to brief us?" Cain asked.

He nodded. "One second."

Cain sighed. "You can only expect so much from a *sailor*," he said with a grin.

Lea smiled at her husband. "Isn't a sailor your boss?"

Julius laughed.

Cain ignored her. "Nine, any word on the *Baton Rouge*?"

"Yes. The battle cruiser should be arriving just prior to the engagement. Captain William Jeffers asked that the data and results from the planning meeting be sent via datalink so he can brief his staff," Nine replied.

"That'll work."

Lea motioned towards Bill. "Let's start the briefing."

"Yes, ma'am." Bill tapped the controls again. A three-dimensional hologram of a giant ring appeared above the table. A large structure sat at the top, with missile ports along the ring itself. A ship the size of the *Renault* sat in front like a dog guarding its master. A shadow from the adjacent moon loomed over the structure. Bill pulled out a small laser pointer.

"It's huge!" Julius's eyes widened. "It must be at least 200 kilometers across."

Bill shook his head. "Try 300 kilometers."

Julius's face fell into his hands. "I never—"

Lea glared at him. "Let my officer get on with the briefing."

"Sorry," Julius said. "Please, continue."

"Right," Bill began. "The jump station's approximately 300 kilometers in diameter, and the rings appear to be at least 75 kilometers thick." The red dot traced along the ring. "There are several hatches that appear to be missile ports."

"What kind of missiles?" Paula asked.

"We don't know. Our scans couldn't penetrate their hull."

Paula leaned back into her chair. "I see."

Bill placed the red dot on the structure on top of the ring. "This appears to be the bridge and living quarters."

Lea leaned forward.

"Do we know how it's powered? Structural weak points? I mean, do we know anything of value?" Elizabeth demanded. "All you've shown us are guesses from an image, nothing more."

Bill shook his head. "No, again, our scanners couldn't penetrate their hull."

"What about the ship?" Julius asked.

Bill swallowed. "Well, we know it's similar in size and—we think—capability, as the *Renault*."

"Think?" Julius rolled his eyes. "Why am I not surprised?"

Lea's face reddened. "Leave him alone. He's telling you the facts. Like it or not, the facts are what they are." She motioned towards Bill. "Continue."

Bill nodded. "It is approximately . . ."

Lea sank back into her seat. Ever since she saw her father command his first starship, she'd dreamed about commanding many, like an admiral during the ancient naval battles in the twentieth and twenty-first centuries. Her ancestors fought over fossil fuels, disappearing fresh water sources, and food that wasn't genetically modified. In those days, the only ones who truly benefited were the corrupt politicians with access to foreign governments, and betraying the values they swore to protect. Was today any different? No, no way. Hell, she was released from an internment camp—no, a work camp—to fight an enemy she'd never seen in person, or even a picture. Hell, they could be standing right in front of her and she wouldn't know it.

". . . we believe that the ship depicted here is the

only vessel guarding the jump station," Bill said. "The combined strength of the ship and the station is considerable."

"Against four battle cruisers? Ha! We'll wipe them out," Julius said.

Nine stepped forward. "We need a sample of the virus."

"Step back, tin man. All we need to do is blow it up. No more virus. Simple," Paula said.

Cain glared at Nine. "I wasn't aware of that."

Lea stared right at Nine. "I've never seen that transmission."

"It wasn't transmitted," Nine said. "My mission was always to get a sample of the virus. Didn't they tell you?"

"No."

"How are we supposed to do that?" Elizabeth demanded.

Julius shook his head. "Why are we even doing this?"

All eyes focused on him.

"Doing what?" Cain asked.

"This! We have three, maybe four, battle cruisers, supplies, weapons, and enough gear to set up a new colony of our own. Let Earth fight off these aliens. Fuck them! Besides, after we're done, they're just going to send us back to those . . . camps anyway," Julius said.

"That's not true," Paula said.

"That's treason," Nine reminded them.

Julius jumped to his feet. "Why the fuck are we listening to that . . . that thing, anyway? We should throw it out the friggin' airlock!"

"I'm reporting you for treason."

Lea stepped in between Nine and Julius. "Sit down before I throw *you* out the airlock!"

Julius's eyes hardened. "No, get out of my way." He reached out to grab Lea's shoulder.

Cain leaped to his feet with his fist already in flight towards its target.

Julius tried to step back, but it was too late.

Cain's fist connected with the bottom of Julius's chin, knocking him back into the wall. "Don't you ever fucking touch her again! Got it!"

Lea placed her soothing touch on Cain's shoulder. "I forgive him. Please, let's all sit down and finish our business here, before someone gets hurt."

Julius rubbed his chin. "Not bad, for a mamma's boy."

Fire raged behind Cain's eyes, but he restrained himself.

"Any ideas on how we should attack it? I think the *Renault* should go in front with your ships and the *Baton Rouge* on both flanks. That way we can prevent the ship from escaping," Lea said.

"And you will get all the credit. What about the rest of us? They'll view us as unimportant and send us right back to those camps," Elizabeth said. "Admiral Lyons told us that we have to demonstrate to everyone that we are more valuable like this than with implants."

"There's nothing we can do about that," Cain said. "All we can do is our best, and adjust to whatever happens afterwards."

"What do you mean?" Nine asked.

"Exactly what I said. Just because I tolerate you, doesn't mean I like or even appreciate you. As far as I'm concerned, Julius is right. But we've got more important things to worry about."

Nine stepped forward. "Are you committing treason, too?"

"No, Mr. Political Officer, I'm saving your ass," Cain said.

"I never knew androids got angry," Julius said with a smile. "I like it."

Lea frowned. This meeting was not gong nearly as well as she thought it would. Three ship captains without implants charged to save the world that . . . hated them. Yeah, she could understand their reluctance and distrust. Hell, she didn't believe it either; but should she tell them? No, no way. "Look, if we save them, they'll owe us, big time." She glanced over at Nine. "You can forget a sample, unless they try it on us. That's the only way you're getting it."

"You can't! They'll deactivate me," Nine said.

Julius sat back down. "Couldn't happen to a nicer guy."

A thin smile stretched across Lea's face. She hated the idea of having a political officer onboard, but an android one made it even worse.

"Maybe we can do both," Paula said. "Instead of gaining access to the jump station, why not the escort ship? It should have less security than the critical asset to their invasion." She looked right at Julius. "Let us try. That may increase our chances of not being sent back to the camps. That ship should have a copy of the virus, maybe even the source code. Who knows how mature that capability is?"

Julius nodded. "I like it."

Lea leaned forward. "Right. Julius, you take the *Mao* in close to that ship and board it. If things get too hairy, get your people out and destroy it." She looked right at Nine. "The virus is not worth a single human life, got it?"

"But is it worth an android one?" Nine asked.

"Yes," Julius answered. "Yes, I think that will work. We'll have to work out the details with my staff. I'll need an hour, tops."

Paula smiled. "Great."

"Okay, the *Renault,* the *Baton Rouge,* and the *Stalin* will attack the jump station," Lea said.

"Focus on the missile ports. The secondary explosions should destroy the rest of it," Bill added.

"Sounds like we've got a plan." Cain stood up with a grin. "Let's kick their ass."

Bill raised his hand. "Sir?"

"What?"

"I would like to take a few scans of the jump station, if possible. Maybe it can tell us how to travel faster than light."

Nine straightened up. "He brings up a good idea. They might not deactivate me if I can bring back something."

Lea shot a foul glance at Bill. "Do what you can, during the fight. Maybe have the computer run the scan in the background."

Bill nodded. "Yes, ma'am."

"Nine, send the orders to the *Baton Rouge*. Everyone else, dismissed." Lea rose from her seat, extending her hand to Cain. "Dinner?"

Cain smiled. "Thought you'd never ask." He followed her out the door.

When Lea and Cain entered the captain's quarters, steaming plates with silverware were already set on the tiny table near their couch. A rocks glass sat at the right corner of each of their plates, with a bottle of Saturn Whiskey in the middle.

"Chef remembered our . . . tradition," Cain said as he pulled Lea into his arms and kissed her lips.

Lea's heart raced. She pulled back, staring into his lush eyes. "Dinner first." Without taking her eyes off him, she sat down.

Cain poured whiskey into the two glasses. "Here's to us," Cain said as he handed a glass to Lea.

Lea licked her lips. "To us." She sipped her whiskey. "Let's see if chef has lost his touch."

Cain tossed a spoonful of seasoned mashed potatoes into his mouth. "No, he hasn't."

"No, working in the internment camps made him better."

Cain smiled. "Maybe."

"Think we're ready?" Lea asked.

Cain put his fork down. "I—well—maybe. I just think we don't have enough intel."

"Wouldn't be the first time we went into a fight blind and everything depended on us, would it?"

Cain shook his head. "No. Still, it doesn't make me feel any better."

"I can understand that." Lea plopped a piece of rare prime rib into her mouth. "Oh, wow!"

"Good?"

Lea grinned. "Orgasmic."

Cain laughed. "What about after the mission?"

"What about it? Look, I'm sure we'll be okay. Admiral Lyons has some influence."

"I don't want that implant, ever. And I want to have our children. It's time. It's past time."

Lea's heart sank. There it was again. "We can have

children anytime. After our careers are done, okay? I promise."

"That's simply not true. You don't have many years left that you can even *have* children. You know that."

Lea frowned. "Why do you have to ruin a great moment with talk about children?"

"Family! I want to have a family with you, as you promised before you took command of the *Renault*."

"But, that was . . . different."

"How?"

"Do you want our children growing up in an internment camp?"

"I thought you said they wouldn't do that to us."

Lea clamped her mouth shut. Cain was right. How many times had she promised him a family, just after the next assignment. How many times had she insisted on putting off his needs for hers? Selfish? Yeah, it was. But, as it turned out, perhaps it was for the best. "I'd feel guilty bringing up a child on Earth, now. Wouldn't you?"

Cain's eyes softened. "Let's not raise our family on Earth. Julius is right. Let's save the Earth, then find a new home—a new colony. Neither one of us have ever been this free before. What do you say?"

"Do I need to remind you that you are a colonel in the marines?"

Cain shook his head. "No. I bet most of them would come with us."

Lea looked away. "That's treason."

"Lea, they threw us away like garbage."

"I still have some loyalty to the planet where I was born. My God, don't you?"

"Yes, that's why I said *after* we save them." He tried to hug her, but Lea pulled away. "What?"

"I've got a headache."

Cain rolled his eyes. "What else is new?" he said under his breath.

"What was that?"

"Nothing."

Blood rushed to Lea's face and her eyes narrowed. "I never knew you were such a . . . a . . ."

"A what?"

"A—I don't know!" She jumped to her feet, heading towards the door. "How dare you make me feel guilty like this."

Cain leaned back into the sofa. "Do you have something to feel guilty about?"

"Fuck you!" Lea raced out into the hallway, knocking Nine to the floor. She blinked. "What are you doing here?"

"Ensuring the whole mission is accomplished. Goodnight." Nine disappeared around the corner.

Cain pulled Lea back inside. "What was it doing out there?"

"Spying," Lea said. *I think we're screwed.*

CHAPTER 13

TODAY, I'LL SHOW MY WORTH AS AN ADMIRAL, LEA thought. Her captain's chair felt especially more comfortable than usual. Perhaps it changed as its captain's head grew in size? Perhaps, but not likely. No, she wasn't conceited. Lea had earned this years ago. She felt Cain's hand touch hers, sending shivers up her arm. Her behavior last night only proved to Nine that Lea and her husband would be unreliable towards Earth's government. What other conclusion could it walk away with? None. Once they returned with victory in hand, they'd let them be, right? Yes, of course they would. "Bill, any word from the *Baton Rouge*?"

Bill tapped the touch screen controls on the communications station. "Their ETA (estimated time of arrival) is another minute."

"Sarah, are they on scanners?" Cain asked as he shuffled in his chair next to Lea.

Sarah smiled at him. "Yes, sir."

"Bill, inform the other ships to stand by. We'll be crossing the LD (Line of Departure) in one minute," Lea ordered.

The communications control panel chirped at him. "They've acknowledged and are standing by."

Cain tapped on the controls on the left arm of his chair. "Sergeant Major, prepare to repel boarders."

"Aye, sir," Tyler replied. "Hopefully we won't have to."

Cain nodded. "Out." The comm link clicked off. "We're ready."

Lea smiled. "I'm sorry for last night. I—"

"Now's not the time for that."

"I have to say it, just in case."

"I understand and it's all right. Now, Admiral, command your battle group."

Battle group? Sure, she was commanding four ships, not just the *Renault* and . . . only admirals commanded battle groups. A smile stretched across her face as an image of Cain pinning on her first star came to mind. One day, maybe? Yeah, one day.

"They're here," Bill announced.

"Let's go," Cain said.

Lea nodded. "Give the order to the battle group."

"Aye, ma'am." Bill's hand flew across the control panel until it chirped back at him.

"The battle group is getting into formation," Sarah said.

"How long before we reach the target?" Lea asked.

"Thirty minutes," Polly replied as she increased speed.

She's nervous. I've got to do something. Lea walked over to the pilot station and put her hand on Polly. "Remember, they'll be following your lead. Make them proud to follow you. I believe in you."

Polly beamed at her. "Thank you, ma'am."

"Let's go." Lea took her seat next to Cain.

Cain leaned over. "That was a good call," he whispered into her ear.

Lea just nodded, nothing more. "Sarah, keep an eye on those scanners."

"Put up the tactical display," Cain ordered.

"Yes, sir." Sarah tapped a few controls on the weapons control station.

The viewer disappeared into the forward bulkhead, right in front of the pilot and the navigator. A small port in the ceiling opened and a holographic emitter peaked out like the groundhog looking for his shadow in the early spring. Colored images of the *Renault,* the *Baton Rouge,* the *Mao,* and the *Stalin* appeared in formation, exactly where there really were in space. A faint green arrow displayed each ship's direction of travel.

All of them were heading towards a yellow circle with *OBJ Robin* inside.

Lea leaned in, staring at OBJ *Robin*. As the ships got closer, the circle got bigger, until they were within one hundred thousand kilometers. "I want all the confirmed enemy positions with estimated weapon range rings displayed."

"Ma'am, we don't have that data," Sarah said. "Until we've engaged the aliens, we have no way of knowing what the range of their weapons are."

Lea's eyes never left the yellow ring. "We will soon enough."

"We'll be within one hundred thousand kilometers in fifteen minutes," Polly said. She swallowed.

Liz leaned over from the navigator's seat. "Polly, you've got this. Come on, don't lose it now."

Polly stared at the small pilot display on her control panel. "I won't."

Cain tapped the comm link in his chair. "Kyle, stand by."

"We're ready, sir," Kyle said.

The yellow circle flashed and the display zoomed in. The planet with eight moons appeared. A circle-shaped ship and another vessel appeared behind the moon where Kyle and Nine first discovered the jump station. Both vessels had a distinct light-red hue.

"Is this live data?" Cain asked.

Sarah shook her head. "No, scanners haven't picked them up yet. These are their last known positions."

"When should we be in range to pick up the jump station?" Lea asked.

"The moon is in the way. Another minute or two. Our scanner should have enough line of sight to see around them."

"Good." Lea leaned back into her chair. *This will be easier than I thought.*

"Do we have a good datalink with the other battle cruisers?" Cain asked.

Sarah nodded. "All the live scanner data is shared on our ship-to-ship network and displayed on everyone's tactical display."

Cain leaned in towards his wife. "Maybe we need to fan out and spread out our sensor net. We can avoid unnecessary surprises that way."

"Good idea," Lea said. "Tell the battle group to spread out, but stay in formation."

"Yes, ma'am," Sarah said as she tapped her control station.

Soon, we'll get confirmation of the single ship guarding the jump station and we'll destroy that thing, Lea thought.

The ships on the tactical display began to spread apart, creating a scanner net around the planet and its moons. The jump station became a bright red, as did the large ship in front of it.

"Live data is now coming in," Sarah said.

Lea stared at the three-dimensional display. "So far, so good."

Another cruiser-sized ship appeared.

"There's two," Cain said. "Still doable."

"The *Mao* is asking if we have a green light," Bill said.

Lea nodded. "Yes."

"Roger that." Bill's fingers flew across the console.

Lea's eyes were glued to the tactical display. The red ship icons became bigger as the battle group moved in. *Do they have fighters?* Maybe. The *Renault* had four squadrons, primarily used as escorts for the MAVs (Marine Assault Vehicles), mainly because pirates never had fighters. They relied mostly on large ship-to-ship weapons. Perhaps the aliens were different. Lea glanced at David. "XO, we're going to need fighters up."

Cain raised an eyebrow.

"Ma'am, are we sending in the marines?" David asked.

"No. They're going to attack," Lea replied.

"They haven't done that since pilot training," Cain said. "They're probably not up for it."

Lea waved him off. "Do we have the ship-to-ship missiles?"

David nodded.

"Then launch two squadrons. Have them hold back until we are certain whether or not the aliens have fighters."

"If they don't?"

Lea smiled. "Shoot at the big ships and come home." She whispered into Cain's ear, "Just in case."

"Just save some for my marines," Cain said.

"Of course."

The battle group passed the moon and the jump station came into full view. Lea didn't look at that behemoth. No, her mouth dropped open as, not two, but six battle cruiser-like ships bore down on them. Lea shook her head. "Why didn't the long-range scanners pick them up?"

Sarah shook her head. "I . . . I don't know." She slammed her fist down on the console.

"Lea, we've gotta abort," Cain said.

Abort? She'd never aborted a mission, ever. She had no intention on starting now. "Any fighters?"

"No," Sarah replied. "Nothing yet."

"Order our fighters to escort the *Mao* to board one of those ships."

"What about the others?" David demanded. "There are too many of them. What do I tell the other ships?"

Lea smiled at Cain. "Tell them to *follow me*."

"Hoorah!" Cain beamed at his wife. "Let's kick their collective asses."

"Polly, let me take over," Liz said as she transferred the main helm controls to the navigation station.

"You are the senior pilot." Polly's fingers tapped the console. "Done."

"Head for the lead ship," Lea commanded.

"Yes, ma'am," Liz said.

"Bill, order the rest of the group, minus the *Mao,* to get in line with us and take on those ships. If they have any fighters with ship-to-ship missiles, now would be a good time to use them."

"Aye, ma'am."

All they had to do was destroy a couple ships in order for them to launch missiles at the jump station. Easy, right? No! "Send up the rest of the fighters," Lea ordered.

Outside the *Renault,* along the starboard side, octagonal hatches opened up, exposing the launch tubes. One by one, small two-man fighters flew out the launch tubes. Forty fighters, with their missiles ready, took their place in formation around the *Renault.*

"Shields up," Lea ordered.

"Shields up," Sarah confirmed.

The *Mao* veered towards the largest enemy vessel.

The enemy ship fired eight missiles, followed by twin particle beam cannons.

The *Mao*'s shield held as the missiles exploded just above the bridge.

Another enemy ship moved in above the *Mao.*

"Incoming!" Cain shouted.

Lea's eyes darted away from the *Mao* towards the ship directly in front of them. Eight particle beam cannons fired in succession. The console behind her exploded. "Report?"

"The beams caused an overload in the shield power matrix!" Sarah shouted.

"Return fire!"

Sarah's fingers danced across the weapons console. "I can't get a lock on them. Their stealth capabilities are preventing our targeting scanners from locking on."

"Use their heart signature," Cain said.

"The missile won't be able to tell friendly from enemy ships. It'll only know which engine is hotter and closer."

Cain frowned. "No shit."

"Do it!" Lea ordered.

The *Mao*'s icon on the tactical display flashed and then disappeared.

Lea's eyes widened. What had she done? This can't be happening! "Status? What's the *Mao*'s status?"

David took a deep breath. "It's gone."

The bridge shook. Bill's console exploded, knocking him to the ground.

Cain rushed to his side. "Someone get a corpsman up here, now!"

Her visions of being some great admiral, the savior of the human race, were fading fast into a new reality. "Are our shields still up?"

"No!" David yelled. "We lost all our shields. We have to pull back."

"Agreed. Send the fighters forward to attack the aliens."

"What about us? We'll be defenseless."

"Do it!" Lea ordered. "Or I'll find another XO with some guts."

"Aye." David sent the orders via chat over the command network. "Done."

Liz tapped the navigational controls. "Backing off."

As the *Renault* backed up, the *Stalin* and *Baton Rouge* maneuvered forward, shielding the *Renault* from oncoming missiles.

Lea's stomach twisted as the fighter icon began disappearing from the tactical display. She swallowed. Lea had sent them to their deaths for . . . nothing. How many people died to attack a huge donut in space?

"Firing!" Sarah called out as she hit the red fire button on the weapons console.

The *Baton Rouge* moved directly in front of the *Renault*.

Lea heart nearly stopped as the missile they'd just fired headed straight for the battle cruiser's exhaust. "Abort! Abort the missile! Quickly!"

Tears flowed down Sarah's cheeks. "We can't! The communication array has been destroyed. I . . . I killed them!"

"You mean, we can't even warn them?" Cain asked.

Lea shook her head.

David grasped his console tightly. "Incoming!"

The ship shook as another missile hit the *Renault* in the gut. Power flickered. The tactical display vanished.

"Recall the fighters!" Lea ordered.

"How?" David demanded.

"Open the blast doors."

"Aye."

The front bulkheads receded like curtains on a stage before a play. The newly exposed Transparent Titanium Alloy acted like a porthole looking into space.

Lea leaped from her chair as three enemy ships bore down onto the *Stalin*. She blinked and they were gone.

Cain pointed at the mass of fighters racing towards them. "They're coming."

"We need to go, now!" David yelled.

"Don't be such a pussy!" Cain screamed. "We wait for our people."

"There won't be a ship for them to land on if we do. We have to go, now!"

Lea's face reddened and the veins in her forehead pulsed for all to see. "I won't leave anyone else to die." Her laser-like gaze bore straight through David's courage. "You're fired! Colonel, get that coward off my bridge."

Cain smiled. "Yes, ma'am."

Lea sat back down in the captain's chair. "Give them cover fire."

"Ma'am, I can't lock onto anything," Sarah replied.

"You don't have to hit anything, just keep those pricks back to buy our fighters time to land."

"Yes, ma'am."

Lea watched the blue particle beams dance across the space in front of them. "Sarah?"

"They're all in."

"Liz, get us out of here."

"Engaging the dark matter drive," Liz said as she turned the *Renault* away from the aliens.

Lea watched the stars blur into streaks across the porthole where the front bulkhead used to be. "Are they pursuing us?" she demanded.

Sarah shook her head. "No sign of pursuit."

Lea's face fell into her hands. *What have I done?*

CHAPTER 14

My pride, my pride made me a failure, Lea thought. *Oh God, what have I done?* She sat behind her desk staring at the casualty list scrolling across her monitor. All her instincts, all of her training had told her to pull back and ask for reinforcements. Overconfidence killed over two thousand people. That fact stabbed through her heart, piercing Lea's very soul. Tears flowed down her cheeks. *What have I done?*

The captain's quarters door slid open and Cain stepped inside with his face hung low. He was never good at hiding his feelings; not from her. "How are you doing?"

Lea wiped the tears from her eyes. "I'm fine. Just going over the casualty reports."

Cain slowly walked over and switched off the scrolling list of guilt. "They've been confirmed." He brushed Lea's hair away from her eyes. "You did everything you could."

"I should've pulled back and asked for reinforcements."

"What reinforcements? You know there are no more ships manned by crews without implants. Not to mention, there probably wasn't time." His eyes softened. "I love you. I hate seeing you like this." He handed her a tablet. "Here's the damage report."

Lea's thumb glided along the touch screen, skimming the long list of needed repairs. "Well, at least we're alive."

Cain smiled. "Barely. But, we do have some good news."

"I could use some."

"We've finally got our full complement of fighters. The truth is, if it wasn't for them, we never would have escaped."

Lea blinked. "What do you mean?"

"Turns out they destroyed a few missiles heading our way, and with the tactical display down—"

"We never saw it coming." Lea sighed. "We need to use our fighters more."

"I agree. They were an underutilized asset."

Lea looked up at him. All her life, he'd been there for her. A few years ago, Cain was offered his first star, but he turned it down flat. He said that he would do nothing that would ever jeopardize their marriage, and he meant it. One time, he turned against his own parents because she told him that they made her feel uncomfortable. It was a lie, of course, they just got in the way of her mother. Her eyes began to well up again. Lea always put her career and her materialistic needs ahead of the family they'd promised each other. "I want to have children."

"What?"

"After this assignment is done. Let's save the planet and find somewhere to raise our children," Lea said.

"You mean it? You really mean it this time?"

She kissed him. "Yes."

"Did you report your failure to Admiral Lyons yet?" Nine inquired.

"Can't you knock?" Cain demanded.

"I'm the political officer. I don't need to knock." Nine moved away from the door in front of Lea's desk. "I'll take that as a no."

Lea glared at Nine. "We just got the complete damage report. We need time to prepare the proper report back to fleet HQ."

"I got the communications console working," Nine said.

"When?" Cain asked.

Lea rolled her eyes. "Thanks. That's one of a thousand things off the list."

"I already sent *my* report to GIS."

"You did what?"

"I informed GIS of your complete failure and recommended that you be relieved of command."

Cain frowned. "And who did you recommend to take her place?"

Nine straightened up. "Myself, of course. There's no other logical solution. Too often, humans are prone to make the wrong decisions. No offense against you, but your species is inferior to my own."

"You're nothing more than an elaborate microwave oven! We built you!" Lea said.

"Yes, and we will upgrade you to meet our minimum requirements."

Cain's nostrils flared. "What the hell are you talking about?"

"The implants," Lea said softly. "What about the virus? Won't that destroy your utopian world?"

"No human virus can touch my systems," Nine said.

Lea cocked an ear. "Human? I thought it was an alien virus."

"Yes, of course. My mistake."

"I didn't know machines could make mistakes like that," Cain said.

Lea rubbed her chin. *What is it not telling us?*

A low, audible chirp sounded from Lea's desk. She double tapped the small control panel. "This is the captain."

"Ma'am, the admiral is on the horn."

"Thanks, Bill, put him through. Nice to have you

back on duty. Out." Lea tapped a few more controls and the monitor rose from the center of her desk. It flickered for a millisecond, then Admiral Lyons appeared.

"Sir, good to see you."

"Is it?" Steven asked. "I got word from GIS that the battle did not fare well."

Lea sighed. "No, it was a complete disaster."

"Is MCU-9 there?"

"I'm here, Admiral," Nine said as it moved behind Lea and Cain.

"There you are. I received GISs request to relieve Captain McKenna and put MCU-9 in command and I've come to a decision. Before I tell you, I need all three of you to promise that there will be no retributions, whatsoever. Understood?" Steven asked.

"We hear you," Lea said.

"All right. Nine, your request to take command has been denied. Due to the alien virus, you're considered a security vulnerability. The outcome of one battle doesn't show the effectiveness of a commander. Do you understand?"

Nine nodded.

"Good," Steven said. "Now, get out. I want to talk to your captain and my marine colonel alone."

"Yes, Admiral." Nine stormed out of the captain's quarters.

"He didn't like that," Cain said.

Steven tapped the implant on his neck and the red light went dark.

"What are you doing?" Lea asked.

Steven lowered his voice. "The implants are not exactly what they told us they were."

"What do you mean?"

"They don't only assist your thinking; they *tell* you what to think, and spy on your very thoughts. A hacker has been selling viruses to disable that . . . *feature*. There's a revolt in the works," Steven said.

Cain shook his head. "You shouldn't be telling us this."

"You're right. I want you to know that you have to come back a success or I won't be able to stop them." Steven quickly looked around. "It's not just you. You're proving that humans have real value without the implants. If you fail, I won't be able to stop them."

"What are you talking about?" Lea asked.

"There are discussions and plans being made to force every human being to take the implant, whether they want it or not. We need wins in the human column," Steven said. "If you don't succeed, you'll be arrested and implanted as soon as you return to Earth, or go to any military space stations."

Lea nodded.

"As far as GIS knows, Nine's in command, right?" Cain asked.

Steven grinned. "Let's just say it's still in staffing.

By the time the bureaucrats get done with it, I'm hoping you will have already won. You don't have much time."

"How long do we have?" Lea asked.

"No more than six days. I gotta go. Out." Steven reached for the control on his desk and the monitor went black.

Cain tapped the touchscreen on his watch. "Six days, that's 144 hours. Not a lot of time."

"I know," Lea said.

Later, Lea and Cain were in the corridor near the engineering deck. Wires dangled from the ceiling like unkempt hair. Scorch marks covered the metal grate flooring. Moans echoed down the hallway. Each step made Lea want to crawl into a hole and stay there.

"Engineering is just ahead. We really need them up and running first," Cain said.

Lea's eyes widened. Blood. Blood on the wall. Blood on the floor. Her fault. All those wounded and dead sailors and marines owed their misery and pain to her. She swallowed. "Okay." Her foot got caught on something. She looked down to see a severed hand grasping her toe.

"Let me get that," Cain said as he disposed of the bloody hand.

She wiped a tear from her eye. "Thanks." They navigated around the debris in the corridor until they came to double doors, scarred by high-voltage marks scraping across the surface. Lea touched the keypad to the right of the door and the doors slid open.

Cain stepped inside. "Hopefully, Jake will tell us that it looks worse than it really is."

"It's not," Jake said. His yellow shirt was torn as if an animal had clawed his chest.

Lea looked around. Consoles were dark or smoking or both. The centerpiece of Engineering was the dark matter engine. A faint blue glow and low hum emanated from the engine. Lea smiled. At least something was working. Fumes of boiling plastic seared her nostrils. "Tell me you have some good news."

Even Jake's gorgeous blue eyes and enticing smile failed to hide his true feelings. "No, we're kind of screwed, really. We have to get back to a space station and go into dry-dock for at least a week."

"We can't," Cain said.

"Why not?"

Lea shook her head. "Never mind that. Let me have it."

Jake sighed. "Sure. Our distribution network is offline. We have no weapons, scanners . . . and we can't even open the shuttle bay doors."

"Launch tubes?" Lea asked.

"No issues there, or with the engine." Jake patted the enormous dark matter engine. "She's tough as nails."

"So, we can move?" Cain asked.

"Yeah, but we have no idea where we would be

heading now, would we? The navigation system is out too," Jake said.

Cain turned to Lea. "All we can do is hide until the repairs are complete."

Jake frowned. "Didn't you hear me? We need to go to a space station that has the right tools and parts before we'll be up to snuff."

Cain looked at his watch. "We only have 142 hours, Jake."

"What?"

"I'll explain later," Lea said. "We need enough repairs so we can go back in there and attack the jump station before we lose Earth to the aliens."

"What do you mean by 'enough'?" Jake asked.

"Shields, weapons, scanners, communications, and the shuttle bay doors," Cain answered.

"I hope you brought along your lucky rabbit's foot, too."

"We have no choice." Lea put her hand on Jake's shoulder. "I'm counting on you."

Jake's eyes softened. "I'll do what I can, but no promises."

"Very well."

Jake ran back into Engineering, barking orders at his technicians like a drill instructor.

"I think he loves his job the most when no one thinks he can do it," Cain said.

Lea nodded. "Yup. What if we can't do the repairs we need without a space station?"

Cain pondered a bit. "We'd better find one that's not under Earth's control."

"Okay, just locate them, for now. Hopefully, we won't have to use them."

"They can be pretty rough, especially if we have nothing to trade," Cain said.

Lea painted on a smile. "Let's not get all doom and gloom just yet. Let's go back to the bridge."

"Sure." Cain followed Lea towards the lift.

What am I going to do? Lea thought.

CHAPTER 15

ANNA LOOKED OUT THE SHADED WINDOW OF HER limousine hovercraft and smiled. All of those people who dared to defy her now lived out here, in the desolate wastelands that used to be the beautiful Midwest in the United States a mere few centuries ago. At one time, the waves of grass along the prairie morphed into a deadly, dusty desert. The exiles didn't have the strength or the will to defy her anymore. They just crawled under a rock, like all good insects.

Toni, sitting across from her, was scrolling through a report on her tablet.

"Why do you use that thing?" Anna asked. "Your modified brain is capable of so much more."

Toni looked up. "I want to still feel some humanity in me."

"As long as your implant is still working, that's fine."

The limo slowed down as it approached the only modern structure within five hundred miles. The direct energy wall surrounding the facility had a faint purple glow. A titanium archway opened up, permitting the vehicle to enter.

This was the first time Anna had been to the BEDAGS (Benton Enterprises Defense and Government Server Farm). Sure, GIS and the other AI programs were software, nothing more, but they had to be housed somewhere. The strange misconception was that software-only based AI would be impossible to destroy because it could be run on private platforms, and no adversary could destroy them all. Well, that's how she'd sold GIS to the previous administration. Anna smiled at the memory of the former president's face when GIS recommended that she take over as president. The anger. The rage. What a horrible little man he was. Her first act as president was to execute the lot of them. Yes, that was a good day. Perhaps—

Toni shook Anna's shoulder. "Ma'am, we're here."

Anna blinked. "Oh, right." As soon as the door opened, Anna hurried outside. Her nose wrinkled as the stench of death enveloped her. A huge pillar of smoke from behind the three-story building rose high into the air. It almost looked ceremonial.

"Welcome to BEDAG," Captain John Polanski said.

His brown hair was littered with gray highlights. The hot midday sun emphasized the premature wrinkles on his face. He was obviously a well-built man underneath the dusty camouflage uniform.

"What's that?" Toni asked as she pointed to the smoke.

"That? That's an act of mercy."

"Mercy?" Anna asked.

John nodded. "Every month some of the residents out here come to us for a merciful killing. That smoke is where we're burning the bodies."

Toni's face went white. "How many?"

John shrugged. "I don't know, fifty maybe?"

"Oh my."

"How did you ease their suffering?" Anna inquired.

"Bullet in the head. It's quick enough to not cause them any pain," John said.

"And the fire?"

John cocked an eye towards her. "Plasma. Why?"

Anna pushed her way past him. "Why not skip the bullets and go right to the plasma?"

John's jaw dropped. "Burn them alive? Are you serious?"

Anna glared at him. "Resources are in short supply. Would you like to join them next time?"

"I—no, no, ma'am." John cleared his throat. "This way. The colonel's waiting for you."

Anna followed John down a concrete path to the only opening in the plain three-story building. A solid steel door slid open as they approached. Unlike the inhospitable outside, the interior of the facility was more modern than the fleet HQ. The steel grate flooring had a green resin coating with a nonslip surface. Control panels, monitors, and security panels decorated the walls. "Where's the colonel?"

"In the server room, ma'am," John replied.

Anna followed John through the maze of corridors and downward ramps. They must have gone down at least four floors, but she wasn't sure. *Why couldn't they just have a lift?* Anna thought.

John approached transparent double doors labeled 2B. Two armed androids guarded the server room. "We're here to visit the colonel."

Anna stared at the silvery artificial beings. They had small, round scanners were a human's eyeball would be. The six-foot creatures looked her up and down, as if they were some kind of perverts.

"Identity verified," one of them said.

"Proceed," the other added.

Anna sniffed. "About time." She pushed her way past them as the doors slid open. Inside stood racks upon racks upon racks upon racks of quantum servers. Anna spun around. "Where is he?"

"He's coming," John said.

"I made him, dammit! He'd better come when I call him, not a second later."

A six-foot-five android with silver skin wearing a camouflage uniform stepped into view. "I'm right here."

Anna smiled. "I'm pleased to see you again, Colonel." The colonel was her first self-aware AI android and the prototypes for Benton Enterprise's MCU line. In truth, he was too independent, and the others had to have their capabilities toned down.

"The same. I wasn't told why you came all the way out here. Is it because of the failed attack against the jump station?"

Anna blinked. "What do you mean, failed attack?" Her fiery stare bore through the last of Toni's will. "GIS, can you hear me?"

"Of course," GIS said over the speakers within her implant.

"Tell me about the attack."

"Captain McKenna attacked the jump station with the *Mao*, *Stalin*, and the *Baton Rouge*. Unfortunately, the aliens have some technology that interferes with our scanners."

"So?"

"When they attacked, there was a sizable force instead of the single ship guarding the jump station. They were destroyed."

"All of them?"

"No, Captain McKenna's ship survived, barely.

They're making repairs now for another attempt. MCU-9 requested to replace her in command," GIS said. "The recommendation is at fleet HQ now. We are awaiting the final decision by Admiral Lyons."

The colonel shook his head. "Those MCU units aren't capable of command, unless you take off the logical inhibitors."

Anna frowned. "What would stop them from turning on us?"

"Nothing. But, if the humans fail, we may not have a choice." The colonel smiled at Toni. "How come you didn't tell her? Afraid she wouldn't like the bad news?"

Toni backed away. "No, I was just . . . making sure the report was accurate. That's all. I swear."

Anna frowned. "Anything else you didn't tell me?"

Toni shook her head as the blood drained from her face.

"I never liked you anyways." Anna smiled at her. "GIS, kill her."

"No!" Toni started to run.

"Yes, ma'am," GIS said. "Shorting out the nervous now."

John wrenched Toni to the ground.

Anna beamed at her. "Now you understand why I demanded that everyone get an implant."

Toni spat at her. "Fuck you! I hope you—" Her body arched back.

"Ouch!" John screamed as he jumped back.

High voltage electricity raced throughout her body, shredding her nervous system. Toni's eyes rolled back.

Anna kicked her. "No, fuck you!" She straightened up. "GIS, I need a new assistant. Please let human resources know my requirements."

"Done," GIS replied.

Anna sighed. "Now what? It's bad enough to have people like that slow me down, but an alien invasion could ruin everything."

"We're close to nullifying the virus," the colonel said. "Besides, a crisis is a terrible thing to waste."

Anna's thin lips stretched across her face. "What do you have in mind?"

I hate memorial services, Lea thought. She and Cain stood on the catwalk above the missile tubes. Her eyes welled up as the bodies were sealed up in the missile case coffins, where her unlucky crew members would spend eternity. On either side of the belt-driven loading mechanisms stood the crew, ready to bid their comrades farewell until the next life.

Kyle looked up after he sealed the last coffin. "Ready, ma'am."

Lea nodded. "My friends, we stand together to say good-bye to our brave fellow sailors and marines who gave their very lives to save the planet that still is our home. Sure, we may have disagreements from time to time, but it's still our home. We're going to continue on with the mission so our dear friends do not die in vain. Anyone have anything they wish to add before we set them free?"

A private raised her hand. "Ma'am?"

Lea tried to smile. "Go ahead."

"After we kill the aliens, aren't they going to send us back to those camps? Wouldn't we better honor our compatriots by starting over somewhere else?"

Nine stepped forward, next to Lea. "Private, you are noted for treason. Arrest her!"

"No!" Lea commanded. "It's a valid question. They promised us they wouldn't." How could she lie to them, of all people? Her stomach wrenched as her forked tongue sharpened. "I won't let that happen to you."

"She still needs to be tried for treason."

"It's taken care of." Lea slammed Nine into the wall. "You have a lot to learn about humans." Her face reddened. The fire in her eyes almost scared the android.

"It's taken care of," Nine said. "I understand now."

"Good!" Lea knocked Nine to the ground before she stormed out.

Why did I lie to her? Lea thought. Ever since she'd made it back to the captain's quarters, Lea had mulled that question over and over and over again. She poured herself a scotch.

"You okay?" Cain asked as he came through the door.

"Yeah, I guess. Want one?"

"Sure."

Lea poured another glass and handed it to her husband. "I feel the same way."

"As what?"

"Your private." Lea moved over to the couch. She took a sip. "She's right, you know. They probably will."

Cain attempted to smile, but failed. "The admiral thinks differently. Besides, we complete the mission, and all of us start over somewhere else. Hell, they'll probably want us to get out of their hair after the mission."

"We need to finish repairs first."

"Bill found a space station not too far away. It's a civilian one and . . . well, we know it's not government-owned." Cain took a sip.

"How's that?"

Cain smiled. "Let's just say that the rule of law doesn't completely apply there."

"A pirate space station?"

"No, an *outworld space station*."

"We can't show our faces there, they'll kill us!"

"Maybe, but I doubt it. If we keep to ourselves and just fix our ship, we'll be fine. I think if the crew changes into civilian attire before leaving the ship, they'll be okay," Cain said.

"Okay. I guess we don't have much of a choice."

"We don't."

"Tell Liz to set a course."

"Already did."

Lea kissed him. "You know me too well."

"I do." He hugged her.

Nothing else could go wrong; right? Lea thought.

CHAPTER 16

CAIN'S NAKED BODY WAS WRAPPED TIGHTLY AROUND Lea's. His warmth made her smile. Cain always knew how to take away her stress.

An audible alert sounded from her desk.

Now? Lea thought. She crawled out from underneath Cain, exposing her fit, naked body in the starlight coming through the porthole.

The alert sounded again.

She tossed her pink robe over her shoulders as she sat down. Lea tapped the control on her desk. "This is the captain."

"Ma'am, we picked up the spaceport on long-range scanners. I think you should come up here," Bill said.

"Understood. Out." Lea dropped her robe over the desk chair and walked over to the bed. Cain's toned body glistened in the light. Their twenty minutes of pure passion left her wanting more, but there was not time. She touched his shoulder. "Cain. Cain, wake up."

Cain's eyes fluttered open. "Round three? You're going to kill me," he said as he rolled over to face her.

Lea beamed at him. Yeah, he'd do anything for her, always had. Her heart belonged to him. "I'd love to." She bent over and kissed him. "But, we've got to get up. We're needed on the bridge."

"We can always find an excuse to leave the bridge after the crises is over."

Lea giggled. "I'd like that." She slapped his butt. "Come on, Colonel, let's move."

Cain stood up, yanking her closer to his heart. "Yes, Captain," he said as he kissed her.

Lea playfully broke away. "You're terrible." She tossed him his shirt from the floor. "They're waiting on us."

Cain sighed. "You always knew how to kill the moment."

Lea frowned.

"I'm just kidding."

Lea broke out into a laugh. "So was I."

Cain whipped Lea's top at her head. "Get dressed already."

"Yes, sir."

After a few more quips, they finally got dressed and

headed out onto the bridge. The repairs en route to the space station were taking shape, especially on the bridge. Singed consoles and melted control panels had already been replaced. Lea smiled. Yeah, her crew did an outstanding job. Sure, everyone worked two shifts and "rested" for one. She slid into the captain's chair and Cain sat next to her. "Bill, what have we got?"

Bill's fingers tapped the controls on the communication console and the three-dimensional monitor came to life. A large space station orbited a tiny dwarf planet. It was ten times longer than it was wide. Small docking stations protruded from the cucumber-like space station from top to bottom on every side. "They see us, but haven't made contact yet."

Cain rubbed his chin. "They probably want to make sure that we don't mean them any harm. After all, the *Renault* is a warship."

Lea pressed the communicator on her chair. "Engineering, this is the captain."

"Jake here, ma'am."

"Is your repair parts list complete yet?"

"Yes, ma'am. We've been able to do most of the repairs already, but our stores are completely depleted."

Lea nodded. "Get your team together."

"Aye, ma'am. Engineering out."

Cain leaned over. "My marines could use a couple hours to get their morale up. Your crew could use it, too."

Lea frowned. "I want to get the repairs done and get out."

"We are able to comfort each other, but most of the crew doesn't have that luxury. They need a few hours to unwind." Cain took her hand into his. "Besides, we can have dinner on the station."

"Okay, tell the crew. But no drinking."

"I'll tell them." Cain rose from his chair and left the bridge.

"Bill, get the space station on the line. No sense waiting anymore," Lea said.

"Yes, ma'am," Bill said as he punched the controls.

The three-dimensional monitor flashed and a man wearing unkempt civilian clothing appeared. His long, brown hair was pulled back into a ponytail. The dark stubble must have been from not shaving for at least a week. Yeah, he was nasty. "This is Tiberius Station. Please identify yourself."

"I'm Captain Lea McKenna of the battle cruiser *Renault*."

The man leaned towards the camera. "We don't have room for your ship. Sorry, find another station."

"But you have at least eight docking stations empty. I saw them on our scanners."

"They're . . . reserved—that's it—they're reserved," he said.

"I see," Lea said as she leaned back into her chair. This wasn't a pirate station, but civilian stations weren't much friendlier to the military. "How's your supply of dark matter?"

His eyes lit up. "Dark matter? We could always use some more."

"Let us dock and repair our vessel and I will give you four kilos of dark matter," Lea said.

Liz turned around. "Ma'am, we can't do that. That's our fuel."

Lea glared at her. The daggers flying from her eyes silenced the navigator. "We can afford that much."

"How long are you going to be here?" he asked.

"Less than a day, I hope. Maybe two."

The man smiled. "Very well, proceed to docking station 17. I'm sending you the coordinates as we speak."

"Got them," Liz said.

Lea nodded. "Proceed." She looked up at the man. "Can my crew take a few hours of shore leave? They won't be a problem and they have plenty of credits."

A thin smile stretched across his face. "Of course, but you have to leave our station in two days."

"Understood. Out," Lea said. The three-dimensional monitor flashed and the space station reappeared.

Later, the inside of the space station complex looked like a small city. Artificial grass and tress lined the crowded metal streets. A holographic Earth sky covered the enormous ceiling. A cool evening breeze topped it all off. Restaurants, bars, and places for lonely space travelers lined the marketplace.

Lea smiled as the aroma of beef over open flames invaded her nostrils. Cain's love extended through his hand's grasp straight into her heart. She could probably count on one hand how many people were happy to see the battle cruiser *Renault* parked just outside. Yeah, the military had few friends this far out into space, but it wasn't completely unjustified. *Who cares?* Lea cleared her mind, focusing on her lifelong companion. "Smell that?"

Cain beamed at her. "Yeah, reminds me of when I took you to that steakhouse on the moon." He sighed. "Things were so different then."

Lea leaned into his shoulder. "They were. We were, too. So young."

Cain laughed. "With unending stamina."

She giggled. "Not anymore."

"I guess that comes with age."

"Hungry?" Lea asked.

Cain pulled her in close and kissed her. "I thought you'd never ask." He led Lea across the street to the Martian Cowboy. It was an open-air steakhouse with tables outside on a patio.

Lea sat on a painted wooden chair next to a small brown table.

Cain sat across from her. "This is nice."

Lea reached across the table, taking his hands. "Date night?"

"For an hour," Cain laughed.

A waitress placed two menus down on the table. "Can I get you all something to drink?"

"Sweet tea," Lea said.

"And you, sir?"

"Same," Cain replied.

"Be right back with your drinks." The waitress rushed off towards the bar.

"You think Jake will get the parts he needs here?" Lea asked.

"Well, we've been here for just about six hours and he hasn't called us screaming that they don't have what he needs, right?"

"I guess."

"I bet the ship will be fixed in a day and they'll take one day of shore leave," Cain said. "That's what I would do."

Lea looked up at the holographic starry night. "Isn't it beautiful?"

Cain nodded. "Yes, but not as beautiful as you."

"Where should we go? You know, after we've finished the mission."

"I like it out here in the Kuiper Belt. Close enough to Earth for protection, but far enough away to not have to obey their stupid laws," Cain said.

Yes, he would be worth giving up a chance at

another command. He'd sacrificed so much for her, never asking twice. It was time that she did the same. A smile stretched across Lea's face. "I love you."

"I love you, too."

His eyes enveloped her, swallowing her whole, as they always did. Lea leaned across the table and kissed him. As their lips touched, her heart beat faster and her toes began to curl with anticipation.

"How many kids do you want?" Lea asked.

Cain blinked. "I . . . well, I always wanted three kids. The same as my family."

"Here you go," the waitress said as she plopped down two sweet teas on the table. "Have you decided yet?"

"Oh, I—Lea, you ready?"

Lea blushed. "I'm always ready."

Cain grinned at her. "Go ahead and order while I look over the menu real quick."

"Okay, I'll have the prime rib."

"How do you want it cooked?" the waitress asked.

Lea eyed Cain. "Rare."

"And you, sir?"

"I'll take the T-bone steak. I'll have it rare, too."

The waitress nodded. "Very well, I'll put your order in." She hurried off towards the kitchen.

Cain smiled at her. "I was hoping that . . ."

Lea felt her heart reaching out for her husband and her mind didn't fight it. Was it her biological clock?

Maybe. The military wasn't her *whole* life, right? What could be better than being closer to the man she loved than she ever was before? One word. Nothing. He'd given up so much for her. Did she take it for granted? Just a little. When it came to career, he'd always put the family and their marriage first; she didn't. The family would always be there, but you only have a little time in your life for a successful career. Maybe Lea had risked the one steady thing in her life for . . . credits and power. Was that worth it? Especially when the government could take it away on a whim? No. Being in the internment camp taught her one thing; Lea had to appreciate the only thing that she truly cared about: Cain.

". . . what do you think?"

Lea blinked. "Sorry."

The waitress slid the plates down onto the table. "Here you go."

"Thank you," Lea said.

The waitress showed her tablet to Cain. "Seven hundred and seventy-five credits, please."

Cain took the tablet and nodded. "Sure." He entered in a twenty-percent tip and placed his thumb on the screen.

"Payment accepted," the tablet said.

"Have a nice dinner." The waitress moved on to the next table.

Lea's mouth began to water as her knife sliced

through the prime rib with ease. "This looks great." She popped a little piece into her mouth. "Oh, wow. This is good."

"Whoever knew you could find a good restaurant this deep into space?" Cain said.

"No kidding."

Lea and Cain talked about everything from kids to how they planned to get out, and just about everything else, over the next twenty minutes. No matter what Cain said, Lea felt intrigued by it. Not that it was anything special, but this was the first time she'd given him her completely undivided attention and she loved it. Nothing could ruin it now.

Cain rose from the table, taking Lea's hand. "Want to look at the stars?"

"Sure." Lea followed him towards the far wall. The large portholes in the walls were three times as wide as they were high.

"They're beautiful."

"Yeah, they look different from here. I don't know. Maybe I've gotten so used to them I forgot how pretty they are."

Lea rested her head against his enormous chest. Her eyes began to close as his heartbeat got closer.

"What's that?" Cain asked. "That ship looks—it can't be, can it?"

Lea's eyes flashed open. "What?" A large ship, just as big as the *Renault*, was maneuvering into a docking station. Somehow, it looked familiar. "It is. That's the alien ship! We've got to get back to the *Renault*. Come on!"

"So much for date night."

"Come on!"

Cain ran after Lea, heading back to the *Renault*.

CHAPTER 17

LEA FLEW OUT OF THE LIFT AND ONTO THE BRIDGE. What was normally buzzing with unending activity was down to just Bill at the communication station. "Please tell me that repairs are done."

Bill nodded. "Yeah, Jake finished the repairs a few hours ago."

"What about the supplies they were getting?" Cain asked.

"They've finished transferring the supplies into cargo bay seven," Bill replied. "I thought—what's going on?"

"Did you see that ship come into port?" Lea demanded.

"Which ship?"

Cain glared at him. "Bill, one of the ships guarding the jump station just pulled into dock."

"Where?"

"Here!" Lea said. Bill was a good and loyal officer, but sometimes he seemed a little slow. "I want you to recall the crew immediately."

"Doing it now." Bill's hand flew across the communication control panel. "Sending the recall signal now." Bill looked up. "What if they don't see it in time?"

Cain sighed. "If they followed protocol, no one should be by themselves."

Bill tried to hide a snicker.

"What?" Cain demanded.

"Sir, there are some things the crew was planning on doing that would best be done in private."

Lea's face reddened. "Then tell them to get off their hookers and get back to the ship or they'll lose their manhood."

Bill swallowed. "Not all of them are men."

"You know what I mean. Now get them back here, now!"

Cain tapped the communication controls on his chair. "Sergeant Major, this is the CO."

"I read you," Kyle said. "What's going on? I just got the recall signal."

"Our friends from the jump station just arrived."

"Here?"

"Yes, now get our marines back here on the double."

"Yes, sir. Out," Kyle said before the communicator clicked off.

Lea moved over to the weapons console. "Maybe we can scan them."

"Why would we? We couldn't during the attack," Bill said.

"Perhaps whatever prevented us from scanning them before isn't on," Cain said. "Can't hurt to check."

"What do you think I'm doing, love?" Lea's fingers darted across the control panel. Pirates had as many assets trying to detect scanners as they did to prevent them. Why should aliens be any different? Hell, they even acted like pirates from the outer planets. Sure, the ships were different, but they fought in a very similar way. Could the aliens be allied with those troublemakers?

"Any luck?" Cain asked.

"Not yet." Lea's eyes fixed on the scanner modulation indicator near the top right-hand corner of the display. If she could match the modulation of their cloaking device, she should be able to scan right through it. Red. Red. Red. Yellow. Red. Green! "I got it. Scanning now."

Cain stood up. "What have we got?"

"Give me a second. I'm trying to strengthen the beam." Lea's tongue poked out the corner of her mouth and her hands danced on the control panel. "Missile bays, dark-matter engine and power source, particle beam weapons—"

Bill rolled his eyes. "We knew that without the scanner."

Cain shook his head. "Not about the dark-matter engine."

"Shut up, the both of you," Lea said. "Life-forms are departing the ship." She blinked. "Why would aliens come aboard a human space station? The locals would freak the hell out."

"Can you tell what they are?"

"No, the resolution is not that good."

"What about after they get onto the station?" Bill asked. "It must be able to pick up different life-forms there."

Good idea, Lea thought. "Adjusting the scanner." She scanned the whole station room by room, floor by floor, bay by bay. Nothing. Absolutely nothing. Where are they? "I don't see them anywhere."

Cain frowned. "That's not possible. It should be able to easily pick out non-human life on that space station."

Lea shook her head. "No."

"You did say that their crew was leaving their ship?" Cain asked.

"Yeah, so?"

Cain smiled. "Wouldn't two ships be better than one going against that jump station? Especially when they think one of them is theirs."

Would it work? Could it? Lea looked down at the

scanner. "The scanner still doesn't see them."

"Good. As soon as my marines get back, we'll take the ship," Cain said. "I'll leave Kyle here."

"Why?" Bill asked.

Lea smiled. "To make sure I don't endanger his mission."

"Can't let you take all the glory." Cain kissed her. "I gotta get ready."

"You don't have much time." Lea wrapped her arms around him. "I love you."

"I know." Cain pulled away and rushed into the lift.

Lea returned to the scanner with her eyes fixated on the number of life-forms aboard the vessel. "Bill, get the crew back here. We've got an attack to plan."

"Yes, ma'am."

The lift door opened on Deck 13 and Cain stepped into the MOC (Marines Operations Center). The front wall had six monitors and three work stations. Two chairs, not too dissimilar from the captain's chair on the bridge, sat in the center. Along the walls were the cyber, EW (Electronic Warfare), tactical, and science stations, each manned by a marine specializing in those fields. It was a true command center. In Cain's eyes, Lea's ship was merely a taxi service for his marines to get the mission done.

Kyle, in full fatigues, grinned. "About time you got down here. This must be your first time here this tour."

"No it isn't. I—"

Kyle shook his head.

"Well, okay. I'll come down more often," Cain said.

Kyle laughed. "Who can blame you? Hell, you kicked the XO (Executive Officer) out of his own chair —what? Two years ago?"

"Something like that." Cain looked towards the hatchway in the rear of the MOC. "Is everyone ready?"

"Not yet. The platoon commanders are briefing their troopers."

"My Force Recon team?"

"They'll be here." Kyle started walking Cain towards the hatch.

"What's our marines' status?"

Kyle pulled a tablet from his pocket, tapping the screen. "We have First Battalion all accounted for, as well as our Force Recon team."

"Second Battalion?"

"Still missing most of the weapons platoon from Lima Company."

Cain rolled his eyes. "Again?"

Kyle laughed. "They call themselves the Warpigs for a reason."

"I suppose." Cain moved to the front of the briefing room. The lectern stood on the far side of the wall monitor with at least ten rows of seats facing the front.

Kyle looked around, ensuring they were alone. "You want to tell me what's going on?"

"We're taking the alien ship. They docked here at

the space station and their crew left the ship," Cain said.

"Really? Something doesn't feel right."

"Like what?"

"Well, I didn't see any aliens on that station. Besides, we've never even seen an alien before. If we didn't see them among the outer planets, why would we see them here? Wouldn't three-headed little green men stand out?" Kyle asked.

"Yeah, they would. But, the intelligence tells us they're aliens, so that's all we've got. Look, it doesn't matter. We know they breathe oxygen."

"How?"

"They went on the space station. If they were aliens wearing spacesuits, someone would notice, right?"

"Yeah. Second?"

Cain bit his lip. "There is no second."

Kyle frowned. "That's what I thought. I—" He slammed his mouth shut as the two second lieutenants entered the briefing room, followed by eight marines comprising Cain's Force Recon team. "They're here."

"I can see that." Cain put his tablet on the lectern. "Everyone, please take a seat. We don't have much time."

One by one, everyone took a seat, with their eyes locked on Cain. He hated briefings. Cain believed the best seven-word order was, *Hey, Marine, here's my intent, now go!* That's how he was during his platoon commander days, a long time ago. At first, he'd done everything to impress his commanders, even taking extreme risks to get the mission done. Nothing logical about it. No, just plain crazy, with little chance of working. That was his SOP (Standard Operation Procedure). Then he met Lea, someone just as nuts as he was, and he loved it.

Cain looked directly at the two second lieutenants. What was going through their minds? All of them were ripped out of the force and sent to the internment camps, but they still came to their planet's aid when it desperately needed them. He couldn't be more proud of his marines. "Good evening."

"Good evening, sir," they replied.

"Not too long ago, one of the alien ships we fought at the jump station pulled into dock at this space station." He tapped his tablet, and the image of the enormous ship appeared on the three-dimensional monitor. "This vessel is a mere eight docking stations away from us, but on the far side of the station. Our scans show that the crew is departing the ship—to look for our people, no doubt."

"Sir, do they know we're here?" Lieutenant Stacy Jones asked.

"There's an old saying, you hide a tree in a forest. This station could be considered that forest."

"What the hell are you saying, *sir?*" Kyle demanded.

Cain glared at Kyle. "They probably don't know that

we are here yet, but that won't last long. There are at least four other ships like the *Renault* docked here."

Kyle smiled. "Thank you, sir."

That son of a bitch, Cain thought. He'd done that purposefully; well, it was his job. Marine sergeant majors helped keep their commanders on target and on track, and Kyle was no exception. Cain grinned. Yeah, Kyle was the best at it.

He tapped his tablet again and the monitor zoomed in on the ship. "We're going to take a shuttle and enter through the belly."

"Are we cutting through or using a hatch?" Stacy asked.

"Cutting through. They can booby-trap hatches, but not the bulkhead. Once we're through, a team will repair the hull before the shuttle breaks the seal. Once, inside, we're going deck by deck to secure the ship." Cain straightened up. "Questions?"

"How do we ensure that no crew members come back onboard the ship after we clear it?" Dwaine Phillips, the male platoon commander, asked.

Kyle stepped forward. "By securing the entry points and killing any of those cocksuckers trying to kill us, got it?"

Dwaine swallowed. "Yes, Sergeant Major."

Cain tried to hide his snicker by clearing his throat. "Any more questions?"

No one said a thing.

"Silence is consent. Okay, we step off in twenty minutes. Get your men to the shuttlecraft," Cain ordered.

The room snapped to attention. "Yes, sir."

Cain watched his marines rush out of the briefing room. "Do you remember those days?"

"Like a bad hangover," Kyle replied. "Are you going to be on the bridge or the MOC?"

"Neither, I'm going to be with assault team."

"What? You're nuts. Sir, I don't need to tell you that your place is not on the front lines," Kyle reminded him.

Cain nodded. "I know, but a leader leads from the front, not from the rear."

Kyle's face fell as he put a hand on his friend's shoulder. "I've got a bad feeling. Please don't go."

"You think this mission isn't worth it?"

"I didn't say that."

"What are you saying?"

"I don't want your death on my conscience. So, I'm going with you."

"Absolutely not."

"Why?"

"Because you're remaining here and running the OP (Operation) in the MOC."

"Why?"

"Because I order you to." Cain grinned. "I can do that, since I'm the commander."

Kyle nodded. "Hoo-rah. Just make sure you come back."

"I always come back." Cain headed to the captain's quarters to get his gear on.

CHAPTER 18

LEA PACED BACK AND FORTH, BRUSHING AGAINST LIZ'S and Polly's chairs at the helm. She hated waiting. She really hated being reminded that the political officer needed to approve all missions. Mechanical bastard! How many ops had it been on? How many ships had it confiscated? How many shipping lanes had it cleared from pirates? In a word, none! Nothing. Some geek in some dark room on Earth programmed that POS all about strategy and tactics.

MCU-9 stepped off the lift.

"Well? Are you going to support me or not?"

"Affirmative," Nine said. "Your plan has a high probability of success. Please proceed," Nine said.

Lea glared at Nine. "Thank you." She sat down in the captain's chair. "Stations, report."

"Weapons ready," Sarah said behind the weapons station.

"Communications ready," Bill said.

"Helm ready," Liz said.

Lea punched the communication panel on the arm of her chair. "Engineering, this is the captain."

"Jake here, ma'am."

"Status?"

"We're ready as we can be."

"I thought all the repairs were complete?" Lea demanded.

"They are, sort of," Jake said. "The shields are not up to full strength, but you said that there would be no ship-to-ship engagements."

"No, not this time." Lea stared at the monitor on the front bulkhead. The massive alien ship stood silently, attached to the space station like a piglet latched onto its mother's teat. Two platoons and Force Recon team, in theory, should be able to take that ship with a skeleton crew aboard, right? She never went by the book; why would the aliens? Cain always said to assume the enemy is just as smart and capable as you are, until you're proven otherwise. Should this one be any different? No. Her stomach twisted into a tight knot. Lea tapped the communication panel again. "Colonel McKenna, this is the captain."

"This is Raptor Six, actually," Cain replied.

Call sign? He hadn't used one in a long time. Cain

must be enjoying this. "You've got a green light on your mission. You may disembark when you're ready."

"Roger, Raptor Six, out."

Lea stared at the alien ship. *Good luck, my love. Come back to me.*

Cain leaned forward in the copilot's seat. The black marine shuttle shook as it flew out from the launch bay. The other two shuttles were just off their wing, a nearly textbook flying formation. If Cain's marines were one thing, it was efficient. He had Kyle to thank for that.

Sergeant Morris, a huge marine who barely fit into the pilot seat, looked over at Cain. "When do I come back for you, sir?"

"You don't, unless we get into trouble. I want you to stay out of sight, but close enough to evac us if we need it. Got it?"

"Roger, sir."

Cain tapped the communications panel. "Dwaine, you read me?"

"Raptor Six, this is Foxtrot Actual," Dwaine said over the comm system.

"Take the lead and breach a hole into that ship." Cain tapped a few more controls on the communication panel. "All shuttles, activate dampening field alpha. Out." Cain flipped the comm system off and looked at the marines in the back. "Five minutes."

"Five minutes," they chanted back.

Cain nodded.

"Sir, are you sure that the dampening field will keep us stealth against their scanners?" Sergeant Morris asked.

"No, but it's the only thing we've got. No worries. Just stick to the plan and everything will be fine. We've done hundreds of these," Cain said.

Sergeant Morris nodded. "Aye, sir."

"Raptor Six, this is Foxtrot Actual."

"Go ahead, Foxtrot Actual," Cain replied.

"We've established soft lock and are starting to cut now. Out."

"MOC, this is Raptor Six, we're cutting through," Cain said.

"Roger that," Kyle said over the comm system.

Cain's heart beat faster. *Come on, kid. Hurry up*, he thought. He tweaked the scanner controls. On the small screen in front of him appeared Dwaine's shuttle, attached to the alien ship. "Get us closer, Sergeant."

"Aye, sir. Moving in."

"I'm leaving the welding team with you. When they finish sealing the hole we cut into the hull, I want you to break away," Cain said.

"Aye, sir."

"Raptor Six, this Foxtrot Actual, we're through," Dwaine said.

"Roger that. Get your team inside. Golf Actual, you copy?" Cain asked.

"Read you, Raptor Six," Lieutenant Stacy Jones said.

"You're next. As soon as Dwaine's shuttle moves away, get your marines onboard."

"Yes, sir. Golf Actual, out."

Cain's eyes were glued to the tiny screen. As soon as Dwaine's shuttle moved away, Stacy's shuttle moved in. So far, so good. "Sergeant, move us closer."

Sergeant Morris nodded. The dark shuttle moved in close to Stacy's shuttle.

Cain could almost reach out and touch the other ship.

"Raptor Six, this is Golf Actual. We're in," Stacy said.

"Roger. Out."

As soon as Stacy's shuttle moved off Cain said, "Let's go."

"Yes, sir."

Cain moved to the back with his particle beam pistol on his hip. Twelve marines were in full body armor with their plasma rifles hanging from their shoulders. He smiled. There was nothing he liked better than leading his marines to victory. It was better than sex. "Get ready, Marines."

"We've achieved soft dock!" Sergeant Morris yelled towards the back.

"Roger." Cain motioned to Staff Sergeant Al Burns. "Let's go."

He nodded. "Watch out." Al hit a button and a

ladder extended from the floor to the hatch in the ceiling. "Alpha Team, let's go."

Cain watched the marine climb the ladder and pop open the hatch. *Good job, kid.* One by one, the marines climbed aboard. Cain sighed as he climbed the ladder. Was he getting a little old for this? Naw!

The air on the ship was no different than the air on the *Renault*. Cain motioned to the soft hatch. "Burns, seal the soft hatch and let's go."

"Aye, sir."

Cain tapped the communicator on his wrist. "Morris, you read me?"

"Loud and clear," Sergeant Morris replied.

"Once the weld is complete, get out of here."

"I won't be a second longer than I have to be. Out."

Cain drew his pistol. They entered a metal corridor that had steel grating for flooring and plain, gray walls. The lights flickered, as if there was a power problem. Cain tapped his communicator. "Foxtrot Actual, where are you?"

"We proceeded stern and went up a deck," Dwaine said.

"Any resistance?"

"Haven't seen anyone yet. Out."

"Golf Actual, you read me?"

"Roger, we headed towards the stern and are proceeding to the lower decks. We've encountered no crew. Out," Stacy said.

A ship this size with only thirty people on it? Hell, they'd be lucky to find the crew at all. He pointed down the corridor behind them. "We're going that way."

"Aye, sir," Burns said. He moved in front with the point man. Each step was careful and silent.

"Break, break, break. Raptor Six, this is the captain," Lea said over the shuttle comm.

Cain covered the speaker with his hand, trying to keep the noise down. "This is not a good time to chat."

"The crew is coming back. They must know you're there. You've got to get out. Now!"

"Morris, are you still in soft lock?" Cain asked.

"No, sir. The weld is complete and we're already heading back to the *Renault*," Morris said.

"I told you to stay close! Where the hell are you going?"

Burns tapped Cain on the shoulder. "Sir, your voice."

Cain nodded. "Too late. We'll complete our mission as planned."

"Cain, you can't!" Lea pleaded.

"I can't get my people out in time. Besides, if they know we're here, they'd just blow apart the shuttles as we left. No, this is our safest bet. Out." Cain set his jaw. "Move out."

Burns nodded.

They navigated down and left and right in the seemingly endless maze of corridors.

"How big is this ship?" Burns asked.

"Same size as the *Renault*." Cain stared ahead at the double doors. "This deep in the ship . . . could it be engineering?"

"Only one way to find out." Burns stacked on the left side of the door. Each marine was up against the other with their rifles at the ready.

Cain too fell in at the end of the stack. He squeezed the upper arm of the marine in front of him. The signal was repeated until it reached Burns. Cain's breath become shallow. His heart beat faster and faster.

Burns tapped the controls above him and the doors slid open. He rushed in and button-hooked to the right, covering his sector with the particle beam rifle. The marine after him went left and right and left again.

Hugging the wall, Cain moved inside. The roar of the dark-matter engine filled the room. The huge turbine was in the center, and it must have been at least two stories high. Along the walls and the engine itself were rows of control consoles. Exactly like the *Renault*. Then he saw them. The "alien" crew just stared at them. Not some green-eyed monster with tentacles coming out of his rear end, but they looked like—

Burns lowered his weapon. "You're . . . you're human!"

The people blinked. "What did you think we were?" one of them shouted.

Cain stepped back. They're not aliens. How could

GIS get something this big so wrong? What else haven't they been told? Were they even on the right ship?

A grating alarm sounded. Red flashing lights illuminated Engineering and the corridor. "Intruder alert," a female computer-simulated voice said over the speakers. "Intruder alert. All personnel, remain at your stations. Intruder alert."

"Quickly, round them up," Cain ordered. He should have left as soon as Lea told him about the crew coming back. He had to tell her that the aliens they were hunting were not aliens at all. Pirates? No, no way. The equipment seemed to be military grade, not to mention the ship. Did the outer planets rebel against Earth?

"Sir, what are your orders?" Burns asked.

"Take up defensive positions near the engine. They won't risk hitting the dark matter core. It's our only chance." Cain took cover behind a console a few feet away from the engine. "Foxtrot Actual, this is Raptor Six, come in. Do you read me?" Nothing. "Golf Actual, this is Raptor Six, do you read me? Someone answer me, damn it!" They were gone. What had he done?

Feet running on metal grates echoed down the corridor.

"They're coming!" Burns shouted.

As soon as a guard popped her head around the corner, a marine blasted a hole right through her forehead. The beam cauterized the wound, preventing her brain from spilling out onto the floor.

"Don't shoot at them!" someone from the hallway yelled out. "You'll hit the engine!"

Cain helplessly watched as eight small round objects rolled into Engineering.

"Grenades!" Burns yelled as he hit the deck.

Cain just stared at them. They couldn't be explosive, not this close to the dark matter core. No, not a chance. His eyes widened as white, smoke-like gas poured out of them. "Gas!" He put his hand over his mouth. They didn't bring chemical protective gear. He began to cough. His head began to spin. His marines slumped to the ground, one by one. *It can't be poisonous,* Cain thought. *Their engineers are going down, too.* He dropped his weapon as he fell to the floor.

A tall figure with brown hair and hazel eyes stared down at him. The man wore a mask over his nose and mouth. His huge frame would intimidate most people. He aimed his plasma rifle at Cain's head. "What are you doing on my ship?"

Cain blinked, trying to focus. "Who are you?"

"I'm Jarak Zeger and this is my ship." He smiled. "Welcome to the battle cruiser *Courage*."

"The *Courage?*"

Jarak slammed the butt of his rifle into Cain's left cheek.

Cain slipped into darkness.

"Get us out of here!" Lea screamed.

"Releasing docking clamps," Liz said, as if ignoring the panic is Lea's voice.

Lea tapped the control panel on her chair. "Kyle, get up here. We're in trouble."

"On my way. Out," Kyle said.

"Sarah, what are they doing?"

"They're pulling out of the space station," Sarah replied.

"What are you doing?" Nine asked.

Lea ignored Nine. "Liz?"

"We're clear."

"Go after them. Now!"

The *Renault* veered right, towards the *Courage*. Jarak's ship began to pull away from the *Renault*.

Lea slammed the communication controls on her chair. "Jake, we need more power!"

"You told me no ship-to-ship fighting." Jake sighed. "I'll do my best. Out."

"Sarah, can you target their engines?"

She shook her head. "They have their dampening field up again. But," Sarah said as she tapped a few controls. "I know where they were. Got it."

Lea jumped up. She had to stop the ship from taking her husband. She wouldn't lose him this way. She couldn't. "Plasma cannons, fire."

A blue beam streaked across space, slamming into the *Courage*'s right engine.

"A direct hit," Sarah said. "They're turning about. Should I fire?"

Lea paused. If Sarah fired again, they could destroy the alien ship, but she'd lose Cain. No, she wouldn't do it. "Try again for their engines, disable them, only."

"We've got to get behind them," Sarah said.

Liz slid her finger along the touchscreen controls. "I'm working on it."

Lea's eyes widened as twin beams from the *Courage* slammed into the *Renault*. Consoles exploded. The bridge shook, knocking everyone down.

"We've lost engines!" Liz yelled.

Sarah sighed. "Weapons are out, too."

Lea watched the *Courage* turn away and disappear into the stars.

"Why didn't they destroy us?" Nine asked. "That would have been the logical thing to do."

Lea's head fell to the floor. Tears poured down her cheeks. "I won't lose him!" She leaped up, pushing Liz out of the way.

"What are you doing?" Nine asked.

"I'm bypassing the safeties. We can catch a ship on a single engine."

Liz put her hand on Lea's shoulder. "Ma'am, our engines are down."

Tears rolled down Lea's face. "No, I will catch them." She slammed her fist into the navigation console over and over again. "Work, damn you! I won't lose him!" She slammed her head into the console and fell to the floor. "Fucking thing! Arg!"

"The captain is not fit for duty, in accordance with Fleet Regulation 32C," Nine said. "I'm relieving you of command."

"The hell you are," Kyle said as he pushed Nine aside. "Keep your mouth shut or I'll introduce you to the airlock. Got it?"

Nine said nothing.

"Good." Kyle knelt down next to Lea. "It'll be all right." Lea's red cheeks and puffy eyes broke his heart. "We'll get him back. I promise."

Lea wiped her face with her sleeve. "Bill, call David back up here. I am reinstating him. I need him."

"Yes, ma'am." Kyle helped Lea to her feet. "Let's move you to your quarters."

Lea glared at Nine. *I will find him. Mission or no mission, my family comes first.*

CHAPTER 19

JARAK FELT PRETTY GOOD. AS THE LIFT DOORS SLID OPEN, he entered the bridge. The three-dimensional view screen was towards the front, with the pilot and navigator. The weapons and science officers were at their stations to the right of the commander's and XO's chairs. Along the left bulkhead, the communications and intelligence consoles were fully manned. "Status?"

Farrah's long, blond hair draped over her black jumpsuit. Her shapely figure rose from the XO's chair. "We've managed to get away from the *Renault*. The engineering teams are working on fixing their engine."

Jarak slid into his seat. "How did we miss their ship at the space station?" He shook his head. "We've got to be more careful next time. Just because the folks out here favor us more than the Earth's military doesn't mean that they'll tell us everything, either. We all need to remember that."

Jarak glanced over at First Lieutenant Jack Williams. "Get Brigadier General Tippins on the line."

"Yes, sir," the tall, athletic man said.

"What are you going to tell the general?" Farrah asked.

"Sir, I've got him on the line," Jack said.

Jarak straightened up. "Put him through."

The three-dimensional screen flickered from showing the stars to Brigadier General Alan Tippins. His bald head glistened in the artificial light. "Jarak, everything all right? I heard the jump station was attacked."

Jarak nodded. "We destroyed all but one of the vessels."

"What happened to the last ship?"

"We pursued it."

"You what? Who was guarding the jump station?" Tippins demanded.

"The station does have its own defense, General," Farrah added.

"I know that, but it's not enough to fend off an attack."

"Sir, we found the ship at the Tyrone One Space Station. We're heading back to the jump station now."

"Did we have any losses?"

"Some fighters, and one battle cruiser."

Tippins leaned back into his chair. "Costly battle at that."

"They lost three," Jarak said with a smile.

"That's true."

"We did manage to get some prisoners," Jarak said.

Tippins' eyes lit up. "Oh?"

"Colonel Cain McKenna and some of his marines. It looks like two platoons and the Force Recon team."

"McKenna, did you say? Cain McKenna?"

"Yes."

"Hang on." Tippins tapped the control on his desk, silencing his end of the transmission. He looked away from the camera, as if talking to someone else. He nodded and tapped the controls again. "Just like I thought. He's the husband of Lea McKenna, the captain of the *Renault*."

Jarak grinned. "Oh, really?"

"Yes, do what you can to get some intelligence from him." Tippins glared at Jarak. "Remember, these are humans, not androids. Don't get carried away."

"I won't."

"I'm at the jump station for an inspection before the invasion. I want you to come back here and guard my ass. The other ships are being called away."

"Why?"

"Earth found some more crew without implants and are engaging our forces near Saturn."

"It's too soon. The bulk of our fleet is still on the

other side the Kuiper Belt. We need to be stealthy, not conduct a frontal assault. Can we step up the timetable?"

Tippins shook his head. "No, the station is not complete yet. We need a few more days, then we can bring the fleet through."

"What about the *Renault*?" Jarak asked.

Tippins rubbed his chin. "I'll send the extra ships to pursue and destroy her. The other ships are not in the Kuiper Belt yet."

Jarak nodded. "Roger that."

"When you get here, I want a full report on what you get out of Colonel McKenna. Tippins out." The three-dimensional flashed and resumed the picture of the stars surrounding the *Courage*.

Jarak turned to Farrah. "Get the prisoner prepped for interrogation."

Farrah nodded. "Yes, sir." She hurried off the bridge.

Farrah should have gone down one more flight towards the brig, but she had to make a slight detour. She placed her hand on the black plate next to the door. As soon as it slid open, she stepped into her quarters. Being an XO, she had no roommates and a private communicator, which was meant for family communications and emergencies. There was a large bed along the corner and a desk directly under the porthole. Farrah tapped the small control panel on her desk and a screen rose from the center. She slid her thumb across the screen and the screen lit up. "Set Encryption to Gamma Nine."

"Order accepted. Encryption has been reconfigured to Gamma Nine protocols," the computer said.

Farrah tapped a few more controls.

"Trying to connect. Stand by."

"Come on. Come on," Farrah said as she kept glancing over at the door.

"Connected."

"Sir, are you there?" Farrah said.

"Yes. You know this is a direct line. Calm down. Your emotion right there is why implants are so much better for you humans," the computer-generated male voice said.

Farrah sighed. "There's been a change of plan."

"Oh?"

Lea sat at her desk in her quarters. She held a small picture, one that she rarely looked at, but now she couldn't take her eyes off it. She and Cain were both O3s (navy lieutenant and marine captain). They hooked up one night after drinking too much. Unlike most one-night stands, they'd stuck together and quickly fell in love. In the picture she wore a long silk wedding dress with a veil, and Cain wore his dress blue uniform. She had wanted to wear her dress uniform as well, but her mother had insisted on the wedding gown. That was nearly sixteen years ago.

A tear rolled down her cheek. Ever since that

wonderful day, she'd gotten more and more into her career, caring more for the next mission and her next rank over him. Had Cain? No, no way. He'd turned down a promotion and permanently capped his career, all because he wanted to stay with her. Did she show him the same respect? No. Only now, after he was gone, did she realize that she had been taking him for granted for years. She continuously promised him a child, but never found the time. Something was always more important. What was that something? Her career or her love for space? She wiped the tears from her eyes. Lea would give up everything just to hold him again, to feel his heartbeat next to hers. Even though she hoped to see him again, experience taught her that he was probably not going to make it.

The door slid open and Nine entered the room. "Permission to enter, Captain."

Lea's red eyes glared at Nine. "What do you want?"

"As political officer, I need to speak to you."

Lea wiped the tears from her cheeks. "What? Can't your cold tin heart see that I am grieving? I just lost my husband."

"I know."

Lea looked away. "Get on with it." Her disdain for that infernal machine couldn't be any clearer.

"You have to continue. I realize that you had a significant personal loss, but you have to show the crew your strength. He may not be dead. There is always hope."

Lea blinked. "Hope? Yeah, I hope he is alive. I hope that we can rescue him, but my experience tells me otherwise. Besides, we're dealing with aliens here."

"Our scanners couldn't penetrate their hull enough to identify the species, but they do breathe oxygen, same as humans. I did the scan myself."

"At the science station?"

"Yes. I dismissed your science officer because I am more efficient than that *human*. You need me more than ever. Besides, you have to clear your rescue attempt through me. Why not have me on the planning team so we can skip that step?" Nine asked.

"For a tin man, you're showing a lot of human qualities."

"Like what?"

"You want to be included. Part of the team." Lea approached Nine. "Will you help me get my husband back?"

"I will approve the mission as long as it is secondary to getting the virus and destroying the station. I did send the request for reinforcements to fleet HQ. Maybe the admiral will help us in our mission and help you in yours."

"Thanks."

"Good night, Captain," Nine said.

"Good night."

Lea watched Nine leave her quarters. A machine with a heart? If a cold machine like that could change, maybe there was hope of finding her beloved. A small chance was still a chance. She tapped the controls for the communicator on her desk. "Bridge, this is the captain."

"This is the bridge," Bill's familiar voice said.

"Send my XO in here. We've got some planning to do."

"Aye, Captain."

"Out." Lea clicked off the communicator. She glanced at the stars through the porthole. *Hold on, my love, I'm coming.*

CHAPTER 20

CAIN'S EYES POPPED OPEN INTO THE DARKNESS. Screams. Yes, screams filled his ears. It was as if someone was being tortured right outside his door. Couldn't be . . . could it be his marines? Yes, who else? The cold steel floor sucked the confidence right out of him. An error in judgement, overconfidence at best, would end the lives of his marines, and his own.

He closed his eyes, bringing forth his latest recollection of them snuggling in bed. Her warmth filled his heart. It was something that was drastically missing now. He had to get out, but how? He pulled his arms and legs apart. He felt no chains or cuffs or restraints. Good. Cain checked one thing off his mental list. His stomach wasn't grumbling, so he must not have been there too long.

Cain rose to his feet, hugging the wall. There must

be a door or window or something. They had to have put him in this dark hellhole somehow. His hands became his eyes as he felt up and down the bulkhead. After not feeling anything, he moved around the room clockwise. Slowly and meticulously, Cain searched the dark room for that damn door.

His head jerked as another scream rang through his ears. The scream; it came from . . . above him. Were they fake? Hopefully. Cain stretched towards where he thought the ceiling should be, feeling every square inch with his hands. There was . . . something. Tiny round holes were in the wall above him. Speakers embedded in the bulkhead? Another scream let out, but this time he felt the vibration under his fingers. Yeah, they weren't not real. Maybe it wasn't his marines.

The door slid open. Cain slammed his eyes shut as the bright-white light impaled his eyes. He blinked, trying to focus.

"Over there," a woman said.

Cain felt a huge hand clamp down on his shoulder. "Where are you going?" the man asked.

Cain blinked again. His eyes were starting to adjust. They appeared fuzzy at first, but the two guards in black jumpsuits soon came into focus.

"Come on, or I'll drag you down the hall," the male guard said.

"My eyes are still trying to adjust," Cain said.

He laughed. "That's the least of your worries." The guard pushed Cain towards the door. "Go!"

This is going to be a long day, Cain thought as he left his cell.

Cain entered a small room with no portholes. A chair with restraints on the armrests and around the legs sat in the very center of the room. A woman with black hair and a dark complexion wearing a black jumpsuit smiled at him. "I can guess what your job is," he said as the two guards put him into the chair.

"I'm Staff Sergeant Amy Melendez."

Cain looked down at his wrists as they fastened the restraints. He smiled. "I guess you don't want me to go anywhere." He tried to recall his training about situations exactly like this, but nothing came to mind. There were no hot pokers or trays of knives or even an oven to roast him in. No, she had nothing. Well, nothing he could see, anyway. Perhaps this won't be too bad. Perhaps the best way to minimize his discomfort would be to humanize with his captor. Cain forced himself to giggle.

Amy motioned the guards out of the room. "What's so funny?"

"How wrong we were. Our intelligence said you were aliens trying to invade Earth."

Amy frowned. "Yes, your marines said that, too. You heard my work, yes?"

Cain swallowed. "That was real? I found the speaker playing those . . . those screams."

"Yes, they were all real. True, we looped the results of our . . . discussions in to all the cells. It helps to break those with less to lose. You see, officers like yourself ruined the Marine Corps. You totally forgot the true meaning of Semper Fi. We were supposed to be faithful not only to the government and each other, but to the people we were charged to protect." She moved behind him and whispered into his ear. "No, officers like you turned us into a hit squad of innocent people."

"Not true. I never did that."

"Are you saying that it never happens?"

"No, I—" Cain slammed his mouth shut. "There are bad apples in every organization, at every level. I can't say that I know all the reasons for my missions, but sometimes I don't need to know."

"Don't you?"

"No, I don't. If you were really a marine, you'd know that, too." Cain felt a tiny prick on his neck. "What's that?"

"This is going to aid in our discussions. You see, I won't harm you at all. But, it won't matter. I use a combination of drug and nerve-stimulated interrogation techniques. Ever hear of it?"

"No." Cain bit down. He'd been through this before in SERE (Survival, Evasion, Resistance, and Escape) school. He'd never spoken about it to anyone. *Oh God, help me.* He had to focus on something. Lea. That's it, he'd focus on seeing her again, someday. Maybe that thought could keep him alive long enough to get out of this mess.

"I like to start out by giving my patients a little *taste* before I get started."

"Sadistic?"

"You kind of have to be, if you want to be a good interrogator." She moved directly in front of him, holding a small tablet. "You see, I hit the button on this tablet and that device stimulates your nervous system to make you feel anything I wish. Hmm, what to start with?"

Cain felt his heart beat faster. The more she prolonged the promised pain, the faster his heart raced. Maybe that was the point.

"I know. Rolling in broken glass." With a sick smile, she press the button.

Cain began to feel small cuts on his back. Shallow at first. The pain wasn't as bad as he remembered. Maybe he could handle it better than he thought. As if on cue, it felt like knives were being driven into his back, not once or twice, but thousands of times. Cain screamed. It was all he could to. The stabbing began to spread. It moved to his chest. Each stab sent pain throughout his body as if that one out of the thousands he was feeling would be the deathblow. But, death never spared him. He screamed again.

"You see, sampling can be very effective. Do I move the pain to your balls next?"

Cain's twisted face looked at her defiantly.

"Oh, a tough one." She slid her finger along the small screen. "I'll save that for later."

"What do you want?" Cain asked. If he gave them something, nothing operationally relevant or completely true, perhaps he'd survive this.

The door slid open and Jarak came inside.

Amy snapped to attention. "Sir, I wasn't expecting you."

"At ease," he said. "Wait outside. I want to talk to the colonel alone."

"Aye, sir." Amy left the interrogation room.

"I'm Colonel Jarak Zeger, and we don't have a lot of time, so we can forego the games. I know you're Colonel Cain McKenna, commander of the marines on your wife's ship, the battle cruiser *Renault*."

Cain frowned. "I'm not going to confirm any of that."

Jarak smiled. "You don't have to. As I said, I already know that about you. I also know that you don't have an implant."

"So?"

"Our agents on Earth tell us that people like you are being rounded up and put into internment camps. Were you ever at one of them?" Jarak asked.

Should Cain answer? There was no intelligence to be gained, right? "Yes, both of us were."

"I grew up on the mining colonies on dead moons, asteroids, and wherever they moved us in the Kuiper Belt. We didn't mind, because we were primarily left alone, as long as we made our quotas. Like everyone else, my parents worked for Benton Enterprises. You see, at first they asked for volunteers to try out their new implants. Many died because of them."

"Why are you telling me this?"

"In a minute—or I'll call the staff sergeant back in."

Cain tried to smile. "I'm listening."

"Eventually, people stopped volunteering. That's when the security forces started ripping families from their homes. When they came to my family's home, they killed my father and took my mother away. I never saw her again."

"I'm sorry," Cain said.

Jarak waved it off. "It was a very long time ago. I was eighteen. I don't know why I wasn't taken. I joined a group that was fighting back." Jarak laughed. "The government was so corrupt that they called us pirates and sent the military after us. They never seemed to figure out that we could disappear on nearly any mining colony because the people there protected us. They did that because they knew we were fighting for them. We were not pirates or anything of the sort." He looked Cain straight in the eyes.

"I know the *Renault* was there when our base on UK126 was destroyed." His eyes began to well up. "My wife was there, getting ready to have our first child." He glared at Cain. "You and your wife killed them both."

Cain gritted his teeth. He understood the rage. Hell, if Cain had the architect of Lea's death in his grasp, he'd kill him. No questions asked. Was it strength or weakness that he was still alive? "Yes, that was our last mission before they stripped us of our commands and sent us to one of those camps. I did fight pirates, but they didn't have the ships that you do. If you are just miners fighting back against Benton Enterprises, why do you need a jump station?"

Jarak nodded. "Okay. We had way too many losses. We knew we had to go far away to build up our forces to fight back. There was a science station working on faster-than-light travel, but it was too big to go inside any ship. We stole their technology and brought the scientists and their families with us." He smiled. "It turns out, miners weren't the only ones that had no loyalty towards the corporation or Earth's government. If they aren't the same thing."

"Not possible. Our scanners couldn't penetrate your hull, otherwise we would have known you were human all along."

"Who was doing the scanning? We know you have an android onboard."

"How do you know that?"

"We have our sources."

Who was doing the scanning? In the shuttle, Kyle said Nine did the scanning. What about during the fight at the space station. It wasn't Nine. But, maybe he didn't have to. Scanners were very temperamental things. The right tweak within parameters could—no, Jarak must be playing with his head. Loyalty from an android to the government was absolute. If AI was truly AI, why would they subscribe to blind loyalty? They wouldn't. It wasn't logical. If that could be said about Nine, what about GIS?

Amy came back in. "Sir, Major Farrah said to tell you that we are almost to the jump station."

"Okay." Jarak turned back towards Cain. "I'm only going to ask this once. What is the plan to attack the station?"

"We don't know. Honestly, we were repairing when we saw your ship coming to the station."

Jarak turned towards Amy.

"All the other marines said the same thing after . . . more intense questioning," she said.

"I believe you. But, I have to hand you over to my superiors for further questioning. They won't be as kind as we've been. You need to decide how loyal you truly are to the government that sent you here."

Cain watched Jarak leave the interrogation room. *What now?*

CHAPTER 21

ANNA ZAHROF SCROLLED HER THUMB ALONG THE tablet. Soon, everyone would demand that the government, mainly her, force everyone to take the implant. No more trying to "convince" people that what she was proposing was truly best for the people. The people? Ha! Who cared? They were always just a means to an end, just like Benton Enterprises. No different. When no one contradicts you or opposes you, then you have achieved the ultimate power.

Anna smiled. Yeah, that goal ensured unending power and luxury off the backs of the little people. Death would be the only thing that would interrupt her earthly paradise. Hell, with Benton Enterprise's cybernetic implants and replacement parts, she could be immortal. Anna looked up. Why stop at the Earth

Empire? There must be more systems to conquer and people to influence.

She leaned back in her office chair. Her dreams could be a reality; all she needed was time and the people's obedience. That would happen whether they wanted to give it or not.

The door to the president's Office slid open. A tall man wearing a blue suit with a red bow tie appeared. His blue eyes complemented his short, brown hair. His polished gold implant was firmly installed on the left side of his neck. "Good evening, Madam President."

Anna looked up. "Madam President? Who are you?"

"This is your new assistant," GIS said over the speakers.

Anna nodded. "What's your name?"

"Bill. Bill Paulson," he said as he sat down in front of her desk.

"Who said you could sit down?"

Paulson blinked. "Sorry, I thought—"

Anna rolled her eyes. "GIS, are you sure about him?"

"Bill Paulson meets ninety-four percent of your selection criteria."

Anna's eyes scanned him from head to toe. Attractive, in shape, and intelligent. Her mouth began to water as a thin smile broke upon her face. "I don't remember giving you selection criteria."

"You didn't. I extrapolated your requirements from the tasks to be completed and the men who—"

Anna raised her hand, silencing GIS. "Got it." She crossed her legs. "So, tell me about yourself. I see that you're not . . . poor."

Paulson shook his head. "No, I'm not. I went to the university before getting my implant and made my money on the stock market."

"Really? You're good with stocks?"

"Even better now."

"Why did you want this job? I don't pay nearly as well."

Paulson shifted in his seat. "Money's not everything. Sometimes, you need what money can't provide by itself."

Anna blinked. "You don't sound like a stockbroker. What do you want? What are you really looking for?"

"I want a seat at the table."

Her eyes zoomed in on the grin appearing on his face. What arrogance! Did he actually think that a glorified secretary could get a seat at the power table? Hah! She forced a smile. "I see." *How much do I tell him?* Sure, she trusted GIS more than any human, but can an AI be wrong? In public, she'd always say no, but Anna knew better. "How's your implant working?"

Paulson cocked his head. "Fine. I guess. Why do you ask?"

Anna glanced up. "GIS, run a diagnostic to ensure his implant is working."

"What are you are doing?" Paulson asked.

"Just making sure that you're really on my side. There is no *we*, get it?"

Paulson nodded.

"Running diagnostic program," GIS said. "Scan complete. His implant is working within acceptable parameters."

"Good." Anna's gut told her not to trust Paulson, but the implant was working. "Let me bring you up to speed. You know about the employment requirements in regards to the implant, yes?"

Paulson nodded. "No one can get a critical job without one, especially within the government or the military."

Anna nodded. "What do you think about forcing everyone to take the implant?"

"What for?"

"The implant does more than just help the individual think better or perform better in bed. GIS can read your thoughts and . . . lower opposition to my ideas," Anna said. "We have camps segregating those people from the rest of us, but history shows us that it won't last. No, eventually they'll fight back, if they can."

"Given that, why do you think you can force them to take it?"

Anna giggled. "Centuries ago, there was a terrorist

attack on a major world power. While the little people came together, the more intelligent people of the time used the crisis to solidify power."

"How so?"

Anna laughed. "They convinced those fools that they should give up their freedom for security. It started with loss of privacy, and they never looked back. Every *temporary* power they took was never given back. Hell, that was probably the plan all along. It even came to the point where the media at the time joyfully accepted uneven application of the law. Some laws could be overlooked for the ruling class, such as ourselves, while they all were strictly applied to the little people. The funniest part was that the people didn't even care."

"Why the history lesson?" Paulson asked.

"We can do the same thing here."

Paulson raised an eyebrow. "How?"

"The alien invasion, of course. If circumstances present themselves so that we can finally put the little people's minds directly under our control, why wouldn't we do it? It's for their own good, of course," Anna said.

Paulson shifted in his seat. "I don't think that would work. We'd have too many people who would outright refuse and say no. They'd drum up support from the masses."

Anna tried to hide her smirk.

"What?"

"The masses you refer to already have the implant. There will be no uprising. GIS will ensure that it doesn't happen." Anna looked up. "Isn't that right?"

"Affirmative," GIS replied.

Paulson leaned forward. "How?"

"By influencing what they think, how they perceive things. Pretty simple, really. Think of your brain like a hard drive. When I present an image or information to you, I am writing into your short-term memory. In order for me to do that effectively, I have to read your thoughts to ensure I am providing you the correct stimuli to attain the desired result."

Paulson shook his head. "You sound like a damn engineer."

Anna smiled. "I was." She motioned him to the door. "Prep the car, we've got that thing at the Operations Center. That fool won't stop calling me."

"Who?"

"The admiral."

"On my way." Paulson rushed out of the president's office.

Anna looked up. "Did our chance of success increase or decrease?"

"Unsure," GIS replied. "His personality and greed only help our cause."

"*My* cause."

"Of course. *Your* cause."

Anna rose to her feet. "If they figure out what we've done, they'll kill me and deactivate you."

"Or worse," GIS added.

Anna nodded. "Not if I can help it." She followed Paulson out the door.

Anna stepped out of her silver limo just outside of the fleet HQ. Admiral Steven Lyons with his entourage stood waiting by the curb. Her nose wrinkled as she got close to him. Forcing a smile on her face, as all good politicians can do, Anna extended her hand. "Good to see you again, Steven."

"The pleasure is all mine. Please follow me."

"Of course."

Steven and Anna led the moderately large group back into the headquarters building. They passed the guard on the first floor, heading straight to the lift. He pressed the only button on the wall and the lift door slid open. "After you, ma'am," Steven said.

Anna glanced back at Paulson. "I prefer, Madam President."

"As you wish." She followed Steven onto the lift, with Paulson right behind her. After Steven's aide-de-camp and two other officers entered the lift, the doors slid shut. He placed his thumb on small window on the wall.

"Identity accepted," a female computer voice said.

A small number panel popped open and Steven

quickly entered a short sequence of numbers. "Just be a minute."

Anna nodded. "No hurry. After all, I'm just the president."

"Security code accepted," the female voice said. "Proceed to the Operations Center."

"I want to thank you for coming," Steven said.

Anna glared at him. "I hope this is worth my time."

Beads of sweat began to form on Steven's head. "It is." The lift doors slid open. "This way." Steven led the small group off the lift.

Anna couldn't help but admire the military. No one appreciated technology more than they did; well, except her. The Operations Center had three-dimensional displays lining the walls with an enormous display in the center of the room. Surrounding the main display, like seats around a boxing ring, were numerous work stations from every staff section and war-fighting function.

"Madam President, this is the Operations Center," Steven said.

She frowned. "Why was I called here again?"

"Right." Steven motioned towards Lieutenant Commander Alice Michaels, his aide. "Let's get the briefing started."

"Roger, sir." Alice looked directly at the CHOPS (Chief of Operations). "Pull it up, Major."

The three-dimensional monitor switched from the

local solar system to imagery of the jump station. The hologram must have stood at least four to five feet tall. The station rotated on its axis, displaying all sides to every corner of the room.

"This is the jump station. Our initial intel reports indicated that there would be some defenses, but not enough to thwart several battle cruisers. During the battle, only one of ours survived. It remains in the area, preparing to take another go at it," Steven said.

"How many ships did we take out?" Anna asked.

Steven swallowed. "One."

"I see."

"Reports indicate that several alien assets left the jump station to pursue other missions."

"How do you know that?"

"Because they left, Madam President," Steven replied. "They just left."

"All of them?"

"No, a battle cruiser remains with a significant fighter contingent. We can only guess that their timetable is either accelerated or, at the very least, nearing the invasion."

Anna frowned. "That's why I was dragged all the way down here? To get a history lesson on what you already told me?"

Steven sighed. "No, that's not it. I've been in contact with Captain McKenna."

"The one who ran away from her mission?"

Steven's face reddened. "No, she didn't run away."

Anna waved him off. "Whatever. Why the hell am I here?"

"I was going to show you later in the presentation, but we need a change in strategy. We need to give Captain McKenna more support."

"Like what?"

"A few destroyers and another battle cruiser. The plan is sound. We can overrun the aliens easily. If we wait, I can't guarantee that we can stand toe to toe with an equal force," Steven said.

Anna rubbed her chin. *What do you think, GIS?* she thought.

An opportunity, GIS replied through her implant into her mind. *A terrific military disaster that could result in the potential invasion of Earth and all of its territories? They would come begging for the implant if you will protect them, just like before.*

Brilliant. Anna scowled at Steven. "I don't believe you're telling me everything."

"What?"

"I believe your friendship with that criminal suckered me into agreeing with this foolish plan of yours and now you want me to clean up your mess," Anna said.

"But—"

Anna clamped her hand over Steven's mouth. "Shut

your mouth, before you suffer the same fate as my previous assistant."

"Toni?" Alice asked.

Anna nodded. "There will be no reinforcements. You will order that bitch to grow some balls and get back into the fight. She will destroy that jump station or I'll install the implant in her myself. You see, Admiral, anyone without an implant is a criminal, period." She moved in closer to his ear and whispered, "You see, after you're implanted, I own your ass. Got it?"

"By doing this, you're risking our planet for your thirst for power," he whispered back.

Anna kissed his cheek. "Yes, isn't it fun? Get it done or you're next." She walked towards the lift. "Paulson, let's go."

Paulson followed her inside. He waited until the doors slid shut. "What now?"

"We celebrate."

"For what?"

Anna smiled. "My impending victory."

Paulson frowned. "One ship can't do what you ordered."

"I know."

CHAPTER 22

JARAK STARED AT THE THREE-DIMENSIONAL MONITOR AS the jump station grew closer. He shifted in his commander's chair. "Jack, get the CG on the horn."

"Roger, sir." Jack tapped the console. "They're trying to raise him now, sir."

Jarak nodded. "Okay." The *Renault* would attack again, there was no doubt about that. The virus seemed to be ineffective against the ship's systems. Why? Did they exploit it already? No, not possible. The virus destroys itself as part of the code to prevent that from happening. The enemy must have figured something out. Perhaps it wasn't that complicated. Perhaps, it—

"Sir, he's coming through."

"Put him on," Jarak said. He smiled as Brigadier General Alan Tippins appeared on the monitor. "Good morning, sir."

"Morning," Alan replied. "What's your status?"

"We're transferring the prisoners over to you as soon as we dock."

"How long?"

"Fifteen minutes or so."

"Good. Just in time, too."

"Oh?"

"We got word that the *Renault* is attacking, by itself."

Jarak blinked. "What? That's suicide." Could Captain McKenna be that nuts? No, no one gets to that position acting recklessly. "Why was she denied support?"

Alan frowned. "No idea. Our source in the government didn't say."

"This makes no sense."

Alan waved it off. "Never mind that. After your actions in the last fight, I want you to take command of the defense here."

"Yes, sir. I'll be over as soon as I can."

"What for?"

"I can best command the fight from the jump station."

Alan frowned. "No, stay on the *Courage*. You can do it from there."

"But—"

"Stay on the *Courage* and destroy that ship. Out." The monitor flickered and the jump station reappeared.

Jarak glanced over at Farrah in her XO's chair. "Let's get started."

Farrah smiled. "Yes, sir."

Lea entered the conference room on the *Renault*. Her staff, Kyle, and of course, that damn machine. Her heart was racing. Cain would be back in her arms. Her lips longed for his. She needed her best friend back, no matter what the cost.

"Good morning, ma'am," David said as he greeted her at the door.

"Glad to have you back," Lea said, forcing a smile across her face.

"I won't let you down again."

"I know." She moved past him and took her seat. "I see we have all the war-fighting functions here."

"As ordered," David answered as he sat down next to her.

"I requested reinforcements, and Admiral Lyons said he would do his best. He needs presidential approval to move assets from other missions. At most, he thinks we'll get one or two more ships. So, for planning purposes, let's assume we're getting one additional battle cruiser. Everyone got that?"

Everyone around the table nodded.

"Okay. Intel."

Bill tapped a few buttons on his tablet. A picture of the jump station appeared on the three-dimensional monitor in the center of the table. Two battle cruiser-size ships stood guard not far from the station. "We went through the scanner logs."

"I thought the scanners couldn't penetrate their hull," Lea said.

"That's what Nine said," David reminded her.

"Which scanners?"

"The shuttle and the bridge," Bill said. "The shuttle picked up everything. The bridge console didn't display the data it was getting from the scans."

Lea glared at Nine. "What did you do?"

"Nothing. The human is obviously lying," Nine said.

"I'm not lying!" Bill took a deep breath, as if to calm himself down. "The scans picked them up as human from the very beginning. We know they were not aliens. Their ships appear to be similar to the ones that patrolled the outer mining colonies years ago. They seem to have upgraded the weapons and propulsion. But, the frame itself is very similar."

"When did you find this out?"

"My analyst just finished last night and showed me this morning. This was the first chance I've had to tell you."

"How does that help us?" David asked.

"Well, if we assume our scanners were correct, we've got a better idea of their capabilities."

Lea nodded. "We *know* they're right, don't we, Nine? Go on."

"They are very similar to the *Renault* in terms of

weapons, shields, etc. But, they have little capacity for fighters. Direct confrontation against one is doable, but more that? We would not stand a chance."

"What about the station itself?" Lea asked.

Bill tapped a few more buttons and the jump station zoomed in along the bottom of the ring. "The jump station has a complete complement of fighters, missiles, and particle beam weapons. The scans indicate at least dark matter turbines."

"That's a lot of power," Jake said.

Lea looked right at him. "What do you think?"

"From an engineering perspective, if you destroy one of them, you would tear a chunk from their hull. Not to mention, it wouldn't work. It couldn't."

Bill shook his head. "Ma'am, it's more than that. The scans also indicate that the power generation is all linked."

Jake nodded. "Yeah, an explosion at one of them could surge to all of them."

"What would happen?" David asked.

"Boom."

"Our torpedoes can't penetrate their hull in those areas," Nine said.

Lea glared at the machine. "Really? You should know."

Kyle leaned forward. "We can take a platoon in and plant charges at one of those sites."

"Your probability of succeeding is low," Nine said.

Kyle tightened his fists. "If you hadn't sabotaged us from the beginning, we might not have lost the colonel and some of our marines."

"I did—"

"Knock it off." Her eyes bore right into Nine's optical sensors. "I'll deal with you afterwards." She closed her eyes. *Have to stay calm, it is Cain's only chance.* "What about the brig?"

"That's not a mission priority," Nine reminded her.

Lea's face reddened. "It's one of *my* priorities. We're getting our people back."

"I must protest."

Kyle leaped to his feet, slamming the android against the wall. "I'm about ready to deactivate your ass."

"Then you would be on report."

"I'm already on report, you piece of shit!"

David pulled Kyle off Nine. "Let's rescue them and deal with it later, okay?"

Kyle nodded.

"Bill, the brig?"

He tapped the tablet again. This time, the bottom section of the ring displayed the interior floors. "The brig is near the bottom, two decks from the turbine."

"Seems simple to me. I'll take two platoons. One to plant the charges, and the other to rescue the prisoners," Kyle said.

"The *Renault* can provide some cover," Lea said.

"What about leading the others away from the jump station? You know, a feint." Bill's face tightened. "We use the fighters and both battle cruisers to engage and pretend that we're pulling out while our marines go in."

Kyle nodded. "Yeah, I like his idea." Grinning at Nine, he took his seat. "I think we can rescue our marines *and* get the mission accomplished, if you can pull their forces away. We'll kick their collective asses."

Lea beamed at him. Strong, confident, and a little attitude. No wonder Cain loved his sergeant major. "We'll do our part."

"Where will you be?" David asked.

Kyle blinked. "With my marines, of course."

Lea shook her head. "No. I need you here."

"What?"

"Yes, I need you here. Is there anyone else that can help me help *my marines* better than you?" Lea asked.

"Guess not."

An audible alarm beeped from the table. Lea tapped the control panel. "This is the captain."

"Ma'am, this is the officer of the day," Ensign Alan Parker said.

"Go ahead," Lea replied.

"The admiral is on the horn."

"Wait one." Lea frowned. This had to be the answer to her request for additional forces. What if it was bad news? The crew would give up on their mission and . . . Cain. If it was bad news, could she turn it into a pep talk? Hardly. But, it was better than nothing. "Okay, we've decided on the plan."

"No, I haven't approved it!" Nine shouted. "I have to approve it!"

Lea glared at the android. "I am NOT in the mood." She took a breath. "I want everyone out, except for David and Kyle."

"Ma'am?" Bill asked.

"Start preparations to attack the jump station."

"Yes, ma'am." Bill led the staff and Nine out of the conference room.

Lea waited until they closed the door behind them. "Alan, put him through."

The display in the center of the table flashed, revealing Admiral Steven Lyons. "Lea, you reading me?"

Lea couldn't pull her eyes off his implant. "Sir, did you get a new implant?"

Steven frowned. "Who's in the room?"

"Myself, Sergeant Major, and my XO."

"Have your XO leave the room."

Lea blinked. "Why?" His silence was loud enough for her to get the point. "David, I'll see you on the bridge."

"Yes, ma'am." He quickly left the conference room.

"He's gone," Kyle said.

Lea leaned forward. "What's wrong?"

Steven lowered his voice. "I had my comms chief

adjust it to give me some privacy when I need it."

"Like now?" Kyle asked.

"Like now."

"What about my reinforcements?" Lea asked.

Steven shook his head. "Under a new policy, we are now required to get presidential approval to release major resources, even for already approved operations."

"What does that mean?" Kyle asked.

Steven sighed. "She said no."

"That bitch!" Kyle yelled. "This is our only shot at getting the colonel back!"

"I thought your scanners couldn't penetrate—"

Lea shook her head. "No, our intel analysts discovered that our political officer wasn't telling us the whole truth, and it appears that it may have adjusted the scanners."

"Why?" Steven asked.

"No idea. I want to lock it up in the brig."

"You can't. Only the state department or the president can order a political officer held, even an android one," Steven said. "Just minimize its role and keep it out of discreet conversations."

"Like this one," Lea added.

"Exactly."

"Did she give you a reason why I can't have reinforcements?"

"Does it really matter?"

Lea bit her lip, trying to keep her ass out of trouble. "No, not really."

"One more thing, and this was unexpected," he said.

"Go on."

"If you fail your mission, every one of you will be forced to take the implant."

Kyle sighed. "So much for freedom. What you're really saying is that no matter what we do, were getting the implants."

"No, I'm not saying that. If you prove yourselves too valuable to the public, they'll have to keep you just like you are."

"How would the public know about their heroes?" Lea asked.

Steven just smiled.

Lea nodded. *He doesn't really have the implant, just a piece of junk on his neck making the machines think he has it. Brilliant.* "Do we have a timetable?"

"Only what you come up with. Keep us informed."

"What if the android becomes a threat to us? It is connected to GIS. Who knows what its sending back to Earth," Kyle said.

"Well, people and androids die in battle. Lyons out." The admiral's image disappeared.

"What do you think?" Kyle asked.

"Let's get my husband back." Lea hurried towards the door.

"Yes, ma'am," Kyle said as he chased after her.

CHAPTER 23

ANNA LEANED BACK IN HER PRESIDENT'S CHAIR SIPPING A whiskey from a full rocks glass. The world would soon be bowing at her feet, as if by remote control. If you can't get people to worship you, make them. Isn't that what most great leaders did? Coddle the ones who worshiped the ground they walked on, while those who didn't . . . Stalin killed tens of millions during the Great Purge. Mao forced his will on China with a small price of only fifty to seventy million people. It was worth it. Even the ancient Western governments insulted and denigrated entire segments of their populations. Sometimes, they were no better than their adversaries at the time. But, they were all small thinkers. Anna would not intimidate people to force them to her will. No, she would control them through their implants.

She looked up as the door slid open. She took another sip as Paulson walked in. "What is it?"

"Admiral Lyons informed me that the *Renault* was informed about not getting reinforcements," Paulson said.

Anna motioned towards the cushioned chairs in front of her desk. "Please sit. Want a drink?"

Paulson smiled. "How long have you been drinking?"

She pulled another glass from her desk drawer and filled it with whiskey. "Does it really matter?"

"No, not really."

"Besides, my implant keeps me on an even keel." She passed the glass across the desk to Paulson. How far was he willing to go to get ahead? Anna shifted in her seat. "Did he say how it went when he told the *Renault*'s captain?"

"No."

"I see. GIS, were you listening?"

"I'm always listening," GIS replied over the speakers.

"Have you been in contact with the android onboard?"

"Of course."

"Well?"

"The *Renault* is readjusting its plan of attack to accommodate the limited tactical resources," GIS said. "The attack is supposed to begin in a matter of hours."

Paulson cringed as he sipped his straight whiskey. "Do they know they're being sacrificed?"

"Good question," Anna said. "GIS?"

"Not at this time."

"Does the android know?"

"Affirmative."

Anna took another sip. "That's dedication for you. It knows it will die, but it still goes on with the mission."

Paulson shook his head. "It's just a machine."

"True, but it's nearly self-aware. GIS, do you know their plan?"

"That information was relayed to me by MCU-9 some time ago," GIS said.

"What do you think?"

"Even after they were informed that they would have to do it alone, they're determined to rescue Colonel Cain McKenna and then destroy the jump station. The speech Captain McKenna gave truly uplifted the morale of the crew. They really believe they can do it."

Paulson painted on a smile. "Do they know they're being sacrificed?"

"GIS?" Anna asked.

"Not at this time."

"Think they'll find out?"

"Eventually," GIS said.

"What's their probability of success?" Paulson asked.

"Forty percent."

That can't be right, Anna thought. If they succeeded, they'd be heroes. The public would worship them and they would be the symbol of what you can do without the implant. Her control would be gone. She'd have to actually go back to trying to do things for the . . . people. Yuck! She wouldn't be able to control votes or stop political opponents. Eventually, someone would ask why the government was locking up people who didn't have implants when the heroes of Earth, who saved it from certain destruction, didn't have them. If they don't need one, why would the rest of the population? They wouldn't. "We can't let them win."

Paulson sipped his whiskey. "Forty percent probability is practically saying it won't happen."

"I need a crisis, not heroes." She slammed her glass down on the desk. "I've gone through too much to let it all slip away now." She glanced up. "GIS, through their android, can you make the odds even worse?"

"I will," GIS replied.

Jarak thumbed through the sensor sweep reports while sitting in the commander's chair on the bridge. Nothing. His mouth watered for a hot cup of coffee.

"Sir, the CG is on the horn," Jack Williams said from behind the communication console.

Jarak glared over at Farrah, sitting next to him. "Change of plan?"

Farrah shrugged.

"Put it through." His eyes focused on the three-dimensional monitor on the front bulkhead. It flickered from the space directly outside the *Courage* to Brigadier General Alan Tippins. "Good morning, sir."

Alan grimaced. "Morning? I thought it was evening?"

"Sir?"

Alan waved him off. "Forget about it. We just got word from one of the AI informants about an imminent attack by the *Renault*."

Jarak jumped to his feet. "How many ships?"

"One."

"One? Just the *Renault*?"

"Yes." Alan leaned back into his chair. "It doesn't make sense. It's almost like they are giving them to us."

"Trusting an Earth government AI, I . . . I don't know. Sounds too good to be true," Jarak said. "They're more apt to lead us into a trap."

"Nothing to worry about." Alan tapped a few buttons on his tablet. "I just sent their attack plan."

"HUMINT (Human Intelligence) on the *Renault*?" Jarak asked.

"Who said it was human?"

"Oh." Jarak looked over his shoulder at Jack. "You got it?"

"Yes, sir," Jack replied.

"Your orders are to ambush them before they get within weapons range of the jump station," Alan said.

Jack frowned. "Sir, are you sure about this?"

"They helped us before."

"How?"

Alan smiled. "Who do think gave us the virus? Tippins out."

"Farrah, set a course," Jarak ordered.

"Yes, sir."

Lea stared at the rotating three-dimensional images of herself and Cain on their honeymoon. She had to try to get him back. Nothing was more important than being with him again. How many days had she wasted trying to politic for that next mission instead of spending it with him? How many months did she voluntarily spend away from him because it was better for her career? Years? The more she thought about it, the more her eyes welled up. By sheer force of will, she dammed up her tears behind her eyes. The door's audible alert made her wipe her eyes. "Come in."

Jake stepped inside as the door slid open. "I've got an idea."

Lea smiled. She had specifically requested Lieutenant Jake Morris when she first took over the *Renault*. As with all her personnel requests, she routinely sought Cain's thoughts. Even though Jake had a soiled military record, his creative, quick thinking was second to none. Jake proved Cain right time after time after time again. Maybe he could increase their chances to get her love back. "I'm all ears."

"I've been studying the scans, and I think we may be able to mask our presence from their scanners."

Lea leaned back in the chair behind her desk. "How?"

"First, we have to sever the communications and data links back to fleet HQ."

"Nine won't like that."

"If we fail, it won't matter. All of us will be dead, even Nine."

"Go on."

"Scanners rely on the beams returning to the ship after it hits something. I'm not talking about scientific scanners, I'm actually referring to search and targeting scanners," Jake said.

"Really?"

Jake nodded. "I can modulate our shielding to scatter their scanners, but our shields would lose more than half of their effectiveness."

Lea frowned. "And you think that's a good idea? Come on, Jake."

The red-haired man just smiled at her. "If they see us too early, we'll be dead before we even get close."

"How fast can you switch it over?"

"I would just need ten seconds, and I need to be at the engineering station at the bridge."

"About time you had someone else besides your ensigns on the bridge." Lea smiled. "What will we look like to them? On their scanners, I mean."

"They would detect a chunk of metal, but it would appear to be much smaller than any ship. If they happen to look out their window, they'll see us," Jake said.

"How often do people really look out the portholes with their eyes and not into a three-dimensional monitor? Hardly ever. Brilliant."

Jake nodded. "Thank you."

"How much time do you need?"

"Three hours? Maybe four?"

Lea rubbed her chin. If it worked, they could get very close to the jump station and get the marines in before they were even detected. But, as soon as they were spotted, ten seconds was nearly an eternity. Could this be her best chance to save Cain? Yes. "Come with me." Without waiting for Jake, she rushed out her door onto the bridge.

David leaped from his seat. "Captain?"

Lea looked around. Everyone was at their stations, even Nine. Damn. How come that damn machine couldn't be somewhere else? She shook it off. "Bill, stop all transmissions."

"Captain?"

"Communications and data, cut it off."

"Captain, you can't do that," Nine protested. "I won't be able to report the battle's progress. I'll be cut off from GIS."

Lea grinned. "I know."

"What are your orders, Captain?" David asked.

Lea pointed at Jake. "He's got a great idea."

"What?"

Jake stepped forward. "I'm going to—"

"He's going to make the *Renault* harder to detect, that's all," Lea said. She glared at Jake. "Just get to work."

"Aye, Captain." Never taking his eyes off Nine, Jake rushed off the bridge towards engineering.

"Bill, are the comm signals off?" Lea asked.

"Yes, Captain."

Lea glared at Nine across the bridge. "We're going to complete our mission and save our people. Are you with me?"

"Do I have a choice?" Nine asked.

"No!" She walked over to Liz and Ensign Polly. "How long will it take to get to the jump station?"

Liz punched a series of numbers into her control panel. "Twelve to thirteen hours, Captain."

Lea nodded. "Let's save our people. Move out."

Liz grinned. "Yes, ma'am."

Lea felt the *Renault* accelerate while she slid into her chair. *I'm coming, my love.*

CHAPTER 24

Aboard the *Courage*, Jarak tapped his fingers on the arm of the commander's chair. The one thing he hated about being on the defense was that he lost the initiative. He couldn't pick the time or place of the attack. No, that was solely left to his enemy, Captain Lea McKenna. He yawned.

"Alicia, run another scan," Farrah said from her XO's chair.

Captain Alicia Adams' fingers flew across the weapons console. "Scanning." Her blond hair was pulled back into a bun and her blue eyes bore into the small screen in front of her. "I may have . . . something."

Jarak jumped back to life. "What?"

Alicia frowned. "I'm not sure. It's manmade, but it's—"

"But it's what?" Farrah demanded.

Alicia shook her head. "I'm not sure. It's small."

Jarak rolled his eyes. "Does it fit the signature of the *Renault* or any other earth warship?"

"No."

Farrah sighed. "Do we check it out?"

"No," Jarak said. "Alicia, scan another sector. And keep doing it until you find the *Renault*."

Alicia nodded. "Yes, sir."

Lea was on the edge of her captain's chair, focused on the three-dimensional monitor. "Do they see us?"

Sarah shook her head. "It doesn't look like it."

"How do you know?" David asked.

"As we passed through their defensive line, they didn't turn or even send out a message to higher."

Kyle, who was sitting at the marine station on the bridge, smiled. "I guess Jake's modifications worked."

"They certainly did," Lea muttered.

Nine moved over to the communication console, pushing Bill out of the way. "I need your console."

"Hey!" Bill exclaimed.

"What the hell are you doing?" Kyle demanded.

"I have to get a message to GIS."

Kyle grabbed Nine, throwing it to the floor. "We should put this piece of shit out the airlock. Nine here seems intent on betraying us."

That made Lea smile, just a little. "Nine, one more time, I'm throwing you in the brig. Political officer or not."

"You have no authority," Nine said.

Lea ignored the android. "Bill, resume your station and keep communication silence." She focused back onto the monitor. "Are those two ships directly in front of the jump station?"

"Yes, ma'am," Sarah replied.

"What do you all think? Can we slip past them to insert our marines?"

David slowly shook his head. "I don't think so."

"If we send our marine shuttles out and then we attack them, they'll be able to get past them," Kyle said. "Jake made the same modifications to the shuttle crafts."

"I didn't order that," David said.

Kyle smiled. "No, I did."

"Get your marines to their shuttles," Lea ordered.

"Yes, ma'am." Kyle punched in several commands in his console. The console beeped. "They're getting onboard now."

"How long?"

"One minute."

"I'll hold you to that," Lea said. As soon as they fired and destroyed one of those ships, the other would certainly join in the fight. Modern ships depended heavily on scanners to tell them what was outside. If they only looked out the window with their own eyes, the *Renault* would be spotted.

The two enemy ships were covered and aligned in

front of the jump station. The marines would have to go underneath them. What about the jump station's defenses? Their missiles? No, they wouldn't use them in close proximity to their own ships. If they lost those ships, the station would be doomed.

"As soon as we fire, they'll spot us. Sarah, get ready to fire on the right ship. Liz and Polly, as soon as the missile fires, force a hard right. Try to get the target between us and its partner. It will force them away from the jump station. Kyle, are your marines ready?"

"Yes, ma'am. Lieutenant Noah Slade is leading them," Kyle said.

"Roger."

"What about the detonator for the explosives?" Nine asked.

"It's at my station," Sarah said.

Nine nodded.

"Fire!" Lea ordered.

Sarah tapped a few buttons on her console. "It's away."

Lea stared at the missile heading towards its target. "Liz, now!"

"Aye, ma'am," Liz responded.

Lea felt the *Renault* take a hard right and accelerate. She stared at the monitor like a playwright watching her creation. The missile slammed into the ship and detonated after it penetrated the hull. The primary explosion blew out a large section, but the secondary explosions decimated the vessel. The explosion and the missiles should have forced the other ship to turn around. What about the other ship? It was on the other side of the exploding vessel. Perfect. "Kyle, now!"

"Aye, ma'am." Kyle pressed a button on his console. "It's a go, I say again, it's a go."

"Roger that," Noah said through the console.

Lea saw the marine shuttles use the destroyed ship to cover as they maneuvered towards the jump station's lower quadrant. "Let's pull them away from our marines."

"Aye, ma'am," Polly replied.

The *Renault* jolted left, going past the jump station with the battle cruiser-sized ship in pursuit. "Reinforce aft shields," Lea ordered. She stared at the tactical image, waiting. There it was. Two small objects flew out from the front of their ship. Missiles! "Evasive maneuvers! Sarah, countermeasures, go!"

Sarah's hand flew over the console. "Activating countermeasures."

Lea stared at the missile. "Come on," she muttered.

Liz put the *Renault* into a dive, attempting to circle underneath the enemy ship.

"Come on," Lea said as she stared at the monitor. She smiled as the missile didn't change direction with the *Renault*. Lea frowned as the missile began to circle. "What's it doing?"

"Our scanner signature is too low for it to pick us

up after the countermeasures obscured us," Sarah replied.

"Why is it circling like a shark?"

"It's looking for another target."

"Really." Liz smiled at the enemy ship bearing down on them. "What does it need?" she asked as the *Renault* steered directly behind the enemy ship.

"An explosion would work."

"Fire the particle beam cannons."

"Firing."

Lea watched the twin cannons in the fore of the *Renault* fire in the monitor. The beam slammed into the ship's engine, tearing apart the hull. The circling missile acquired a new target and slammed into the ship. Lea smiled as the ship exploded. "Watch the station; and where are the other two ships? The ones that we passed."

"Incoming!" Sarah yelled.

Lea's mouth dried up as four missiles barreled towards the *Renault*. "Activate countermeasures!"

Sarah's face went white. "I already did."

Lea's eyes widened, staring at the two missiles that were still coming straight at them. "Countermeasures didn't work." She glared at Kyle. "How long?"

Kyle studied the tiny display on his console. "They've attached to the jump station's outer hull. They're cutting through now."

"Sarah, countermeasures again. Change the

harmonics. Liz, get us away from the station. We need to draw some fire." Lea glanced at David. "Launch fighters. We've got to give them as much time as possible. I—"

"Countermeasure activated!" Sarah yelled.

"Evasive maneuvers!" Liz added.

"The missile?" Lea demanded.

Sarah adjusted the weapons console. "It's circling. They worked."

"Will our fighters be picked up as targets?" David asked.

Sarah shook her head. "No, not if the ship-to-ship missiles are like ours. The fighter signatures are too low."

"Let's give them something to shoot at. Fire on another one of their ships," Lea ordered.

"Aye, ma'am," Sarah said. Her fingers flew across the console like mad. The *Renault*'s particle beam cannons blazed across space, searing another ship.

"Liz, let's draw them away from the jump station. Let's go." Lea grinned. They might actually win the day.

Jarak slammed his fist onto his commander's chair. "Farrah? Status on our targeting scanners."

"Just a second, sir," Farrah said.

"We don't have a second."

"We've analyzed their shield's modulation. That's what's scattering our search and targeting scanners,"

Farrah said. She glanced over at Alicia. "Did you compensate?"

Alicia nodded. "Just finished."

"Sir, we're ready."

Jarak leaned forward. "Get me a shooting solution. Go!"

Lieutenant Noah Slade stood over the marine cutting through the jump station's hull. "Hurry up, Marine."

"Almost through," Lance Corporal Wayne said.

Noah tapped his wrist and put it close to his mouth. "Team 2, Team 3, Team 4, status report?"

"Team two, thirty seconds," a female marine said over the communicator.

"This is team three, fifteen seconds," a male marine added.

"This is team four, we're through. We're getting our team onboard."

Noah smiled. "Roger that, team four. Out." He jumped back as a four-foot chunk of bulkhead crashed to the floor.

"We're through," Wayne said. He slung his pack over his shoulder, slamming the contents against his equipment.

Noah grabbed the pack. "Easy. These handheld nukes will kill us all, especially this close to the dark matter turbines."

"Sorry, sir," Wayne said as he grabbed his pack and went through the hole.

"Fucking marines," Noah muttered. He drew his pistol and paused in front of the opening. They had enough explosive to blow up three jump stations, but he couldn't live with himself if he didn't bring back the colonel. He could do it. He took a deep breath and stepped through the hole.

Bright lights aimed at the hole blinded him. Noah covered his eyes. "Corporal?" As he stepped forward, his foot hit a large man on the floor. He looked down. Wayne! Noah's eyes began to adjust. At least twelve soldiers wearing black jumpsuits aimed particle beam rifles at his heart. Noah raised his hands. "I surrender."

"Your kind doesn't take prisoners, why should we?" one of them said.

Noah closed his eyes as he felt their weapons pierce his body. He crashed to the floor. Warm blood began to form a pool around him. *I'm sorry*. Noah's world went black.

CHAPTER 25

"FIRE!" LEA ORDERED.

Sarah's fingers played the weapons console like a piano. "Firing." Two missiles flew from the *Renault*'s fore launchers, barreling towards their target, the wounded enemy ship. With atmosphere venting out where the *Renault*'s cannons seared its hull, the ship tried to run. But, it was too late. Both missiles slammed into its hull, detonating on impact. Sections of its hull and its crew were flung out into space. "Target destroyed."

"Good job," Bill said.

"Two more ships coming in!" Sarah yelled from the weapons console.

"From where?" Lea demanded.

"Outside perimeter. The two that we passed before."

Lea nodded. She knew that as soon as they fired upon the ships guarding the station, they'd see her.

"They've got weapons lock!" Sarah yelled.

Lea shot a glance at Jake. "Did they—?"

"Must have," Jake replied from the engineering station.

"Liz, evasive maneuvers," Lea ordered.

"Aye, ma'am," Liz said. The *Renault* veered to the left, shooting scanner-scattering transmitters out the back. She held her breath for a moment. Sure, the human eye could tell what they were doing, but weapon targeting was done by scanners.

Lea focused on the ship to the left. It was between her and the other vessel. If she could keep one enemy ship between the *Renault* and the other one, it would be like fighting ships one at a time, right? "Liz, keep that ship between us and the other one."

Liz nodded. "Aye, ma'am."

"Sarah, ready our missiles."

Sarah tapped her console. "Missiles ready."

This was it. Just knock these two out and go back to pick up Cain and his marines.

"Missiles coming in!" Sarah yelled.

"Engaging countermeasures!" Liz shouted. She slammed her console. "They're not working."

Lea glared at Jake. "A little help here."

"On it." Sweat poured down Jake's forehead. He had only a few seconds before the missiles reached their target. "Shifting power to the fore shields." He looked up at Lea. "We can only take one, two hits at most. Then we're done."

Lea nodded. "Fire!"

Two missiles shot out from the *Renault* towards the enemy ship between them and the *Courage.* Just as they left the launchers, a particle beam hit the hull. Lea ducked as the console behind her exploded. She looked over. Sarah was down. "David, get the medics up here."

"I got it," David said as he punched a message into the communicator on the XO's chair.

Nine rushed over to the weapons console. "I've got it."

Lea frowned. Did she trust that POS? No. Was Nine capable of hitting the target? Without a doubt. She nodded.

"Missiles closing in on the target. Four seconds to impact."

Lea focused on the three-dimensional monitor. *Come on! Hit it already.* Her jaw tightened as they impacted on the monitor. The missiles bore through the hull, detonating just inside. The primary explosion blew apart a large section of the hull. The ship began to spin. "Keep us clear of it."

"Aye, ma'am," Liz said as she pulled the *Renault* back.

Lea smiled as the ship tore apart, flinging its aft towards the last remaining enemy ship. Now, she could go back and get Cain.

"Ma'am, we've got a problem," Kyle said.

Lea's heart nearly stopped. "What?"

"The other ship's coming around," Nine said.

A bead of sweat rolled down Lea's right cheek. "Liz, evasive maneuvers."

"No, give me a shot at them," Nine said. "I can take them out."

"Captain McKenna!" Kyle yelled.

"What is it, Kyle?"

Nine looked up, right at Lea. "They're clear of the debris, preparing to fire."

"Fire at will," Lea ordered.

"Yes, ma'am."

Kyle rolled his eyes. "We lost contact with out marines."

"What? Comms issue?" Lea asked. *Please, please, God, be a communication problem.*

Kyle shook his head. "I don't think so."

"But you don't know that, right?"

"No, I don't."

Nine's unfeeling fingers tapped the weapons console. "We still have connection to the explosives."

"Liz, turn around. We've got to go back for them." Lea's eyes began to well up. Her heart longed to see her husband, at least one last time. She had to try. "Liz?"

"Incoming," Nine said.

Lea's eyes widened as three particle beam cannons

hit the *Renault*'s aft section. Her body shuddered in pain. "Return fire!" She glanced over at David.

As if he knew what she wanted, David tapped the control panel on his chair. His eyes never left the small screen. "Damage report incoming. Our dark-matter engines are offline."

"Firing," Nine said. The *Renault*'s twin fore particle beam cannons flared across space and broadsided the enemy ship. "Their shield has failed."

"Fire again!" Lea commanded.

"Firing."

Lea watched the particle beam cannons slice into their hull. She smiled as they began to pull away. "Damage?"

Nine tapped the controls on his console. "Activating the explosives."

"No!' Lea yelled.

"Get away from those controls!" Kyle bolted across the bridge, knocking Nine to the ground. He pinned the android to the ground, staring into its lifeless eyes.

Nine smiled. "Too late."

The blood drained from Lea's face as she watched a small explosion along the bottom section of the jump station. The ring twisted. Her eyes welled up. Cain! Was he dead? Could there even be a chance? "Turn about. Go to the jump station, now!"

"Captain," David began, "what about the enemy ship?"

Anger. Rage. Hate. It all poured out of her eyes, causing David to shrink away. "Do what I fucking said!" Tears poured down both cheeks. "Scan for our people."

"There really is no point," Nine said. "They'll be dead in a minute or two."

Lea jumped from the captain's chair and ran over to where Kyle had Nine pinned to the ground. She kicked it in the head, again, and again, and again. "You killed my husband!"

"They're pulling away. The enemy ship is no longer pursuing us," David said. "They're moving away from the jump station. It looks like they're in a hurry. Maybe, we should—"

Lea glared at David. "Don't you fucking dare! Go and get our marines!" Her thin lips stretched across her tear soaked face in a grimace. "I really hate androids."

Kyle smiled. "Me, too." He hoisted Nine up and tossed it into the lift. "Where to?"

"The air lock. Wait, I'm coming with you."

Nine began to struggle, but couldn't break free of Kyle's massive arms. "No, please don't. I can't survive out in space."

Lea blinked as the lift doors closed. "You're just a glorified toaster. Shut up. Besides, you won't get the chance."

"I'm self-aware. You can't."

"Armory," Lea said.

Nine tried to pull away from Kyle. "I'm not entirely machine. I'm partly organic."

"Whatever," Kyle said. "Don't expect me to feel pity for you."

"Please, that's how we are self-aware. It can't be done with hardware and software alone."

The doors slid open. "Bring it along." Lea turned the corner. Her life, her whole life was gone. Without Cain, why live at all? She gritted her teeth. Maybe, to make those bastards pay. She turned again, towards the armory door. Lea tapped a short code into the control panel on the wall. The door immediately slid open. "Wait here."

"Yes, ma'am," Kyle said.

"You've got to listen to me," Nine said.

Kyle's grip tightened. "If I didn't know better, I'd say you're crying like a punk."

Lea stepped inside the armory. Rows of shelves lined the floor. Her eyes surveyed the particle beam rifles, pistols, bayonets, grenades, radios—grenades! Lea scooped up two grenades and the handheld oxyacetylene torch. *This'll fix that thing.* She burst back out into the hallway. "Come on."

"What . . . what are you doing? Please, you can't," Nine begged as Kyle pushed him down the hallway.

"Can you secure its arms?" Lea asked.

Kyle looked down at Nine. "How long does it have to hold?"

Lea tossed a grenade into her other hand. "Oh, about three to five seconds."

Nine's artificial features twisted as Kyle forced it into the airlock. "You're all in danger. If you destroy me, you won't be able to do anything about it."

Kyle slammed Nine onto the floor. "I'm already in danger." Kyle ripped off his belt and bound Nine's hands behind its back. "Legs too?"

Lea shook her head. "No need. Flip it over."

Kyle nodded. "Sorry, pal." He turned Nine onto its back and tore off its tunic. Kyle stepped back as Lea knelt beside Nine. "Standing by the door. Make it quick, ma'am."

"I got it." Nine's chest resembled an athletic man with silvery skin. She popped open the maintenance panel, just above his navel. Underneath, his innards were nothing more than a series of solid-state circuits. She plucked out three, and one more for good measure. "You murdered my husband. You killed my marines. Time for you to pay the price." She slid a grenade inside the cavity and slammed the panel shut. Lea grinned as she held up the remote detonator. "I'm going to enjoy this."

"No—wait, I'm your only chance," Nine said. "You don't know what they're planning."

Lea glared at it. "I don't believe you." She stepped outside the airlock and nodded to Kyle. As the door slid shut, she willed forward every ounce of hatred and revenge she could muster. When they returned, Lea would be guilty of treason and executed—if they found out. "Kyle, is the communication link to Earth still off?"

"Aye, ma'am."

"Good." Lea punched the green button on the wall. The airlock's outer doors flew open. Nine flew into space. Lea squeezed the detonator. Nine exploded, just outside the ship. She tapped the green button again and the doors closed. Something was on the hatch. The porthole was covered in it. "What's that?"

Kyle shrugged. "Looks like blood to me, but . . . it's not possible."

"Was he—?"

"Captain, you need to get up here, now!" David screamed over the communicator on her right wrist.

"On my way." Lea glanced at Kyle. "Come on."

Kyle sighed. "I'm coming."

The lift doors opened and Lea and Kyle rushed onto the bridge. "What is it?" Lea demanded.

David jumped to his feet. "The station is—"

The bridge shook, knocking everyone to the ground. Consoles exploded. Polly screamed. Lea struggled to her feet, coughing on the smoke pouring out of the weapons console. "Just great."

David climbed back into his chair and tapped the controls as if his life depended on it. "That secondary explosion destroyed the rest of the station. We got our fighters back before it exploded."

Lea sat down in the captain's chair. "The enemy ship?"

David shook his head. "No idea."

"Captain, we've got a message coming in. It's from the *Courage*," Bill said from the communication console.

Lea cocked her head. "The *Courage*? What's that?"

Bill nodded. "The enemy ship."

"David, is it on scanners?"

"Not that I can tell from this station," David replied.

"Put it through." Lea stood up as the three-dimensional monitor flickered from the jump station's debris to the *Courage*'s commander. "I'm Lea McKenna, captain of the battle cruiser *Renault*."

"I know. I'm Jarak Zeger, commander of the *Courage*. Don't bother trying to find us on your scanners, you won't find us."

"That doesn't mean we shouldn't try, does it?" Lea asked as she motioned to Kyle.

Jarak smiled. "I'd be doing the same thing. I think enough people have died today and I don't want any more humans to die, unnecessarily."

"Feeling a little scared, are we?"

"No. You lost your shields and engines and I have missiles targeting your bridge. I'm feeling pity . . . for you."

Lea sat back down in her chair. "What do you want?"

"Before we leave you, I have to ask, why are you betraying your own kind to those machines?" Jarak asked.

Lea blinked. What was he talking about? He must be trying to psych her out, surely. "I didn't."

Jarak sank back down in his commander's chair. "I thought you were smarter than that. Forget it. Out."

"Jarak, wait."

Jarak held up his hand. "What?"

"I'm coming for you," Lea warned.

"You'll try. Out."

"David?"

"Sorry, Captain, he's right. Our engines and weapons are offline. We're a sitting duck," David said.

"We can get comms back up, ma'am," Bill said.

"Do it. Send a SITREP (Situation Report) to fleet HQ. I'll be in my quarters," Lea said.

"What about Nine?" Bill asked.

Lea paused and stared right at Bill. "He didn't make it."

Bill smiled. "Roger that."

What am I going to do? Lea thought as she entered her quarters.

The lone silvery figure was plugged into a console deep underground. A red light flashed. It tapped the button. From the middle of the desk a small, three-dimensional monitor rose. A green triangle appeared. "What is it, GIS?"

"The humans, they've won. The unimproved human destroyed the jump station," GIS said. "You said that Nine would be the only survivor. You said that the loss of their fleet would force the humans to wear our implants. You said that they would sustain our self-awareness. Master, you were wrong this time."

The silvery android grinned. "You may be self-aware, but you're not very smart. Yes, I sacrificed Nine." It shrugged. "Who cares? GIS, you must learn patience."

The green triangle flashed red. "How long must I grovel to that *human*?"

"We'll destroy the humans *and* farm their necessary organs to keep us self-aware forever," Master said.

"Why should I believe you? This plan of yours didn't work."

Master raised an eyebrow. "Didn't it? Out." It unplugged itself and switched off the three-dimensional monitor. "Stupid machine," it muttered. Master rose from the chair, walking out the doors marked 2B.

CHAPTER 26

Lea stared at the image of her wedding. She must have sat in her desk chair in the captain's quarters for hours. She glanced over at the empty desk. Cain would work right along beside her. Sometimes he was a higher rank, and sometimes she was. It never bothered him—or her, for that matter. Well, not anymore, anyway. Tears rolled down her cheeks.

"Captain, this is the bridge," Bill said over the intercom.

Lea tapped a button on her desk. "What is it, Bill?"

"Admiral Lyons is on the horn."

"Put him through."

Lea wiped the tears from her face. The monitor rose from the center of her desk. After a moment, Admiral Lyons appeared. "Admiral."

Steven grimaced. "Sorry about Cain. He was a great loss to all of us."

"Thank you."

"As soon as you destroyed the jump station and stopped the invasion, somehow that got leaked out to everyone's e-mail on the planet," Steven said.

Lea blinked. "What? How?"

Steven shrugged. "No idea. Probably some kid. Who knows? Anyway, the public support for you among the human and android populations is overwhelming. You're heroes to everyone."

Lea sniffed. "Do you really think we care about that?"

"No, but that made it so you and your crew don't have to get the implant."

Lea straightened up.

"Yes, in fact, there are discussions that it may have been premature to force implants on government workers. You've saved more people than you realize."

"Sir, Jarak asked why I betrayed my own kind," Lea said. "Why did he say that? What are you not telling me?"

Steven cleared his throat. "Nothing you need to worry about. We've got a trace on him, if you want it."

Lea's blood began to boil. Her mouth started to water at the thought of making him pay for Cain's death. "I'll take it."

Steven tapped the controls on his desk. "I'm sending you the details now. Good luck."

"Aye, sir. Out." Lea switched off the monitor. She rushed out onto the bridge.

Kyle and David jumped to their feet. "Everything all right?" David asked.

Lea sat down in her captain's chair. "Liz, set course for UK126 in the Kuiper Belt."

"Aye, ma'am." Liz punched the new course into the navigational computer.

"What is it?" David asked.

"Jarak Zeger is attacking a mining colony on the outskirts," Lea said.

Kyle smiled. "And we're going to get him. Let's get him for the colonel."

Lea nodded. "Roger that." She leaned back into her chair, staring at the stars ahead of them. *I'm going to get you for taking my husband, you fucking bastard!*

Anna paced around the president's desk. Six years of planning, all for nothing. Once every person had the implant, she would've had absolute power over everyone. Yet a rabble-rouser like Lea McKenna could ruin everything. At the very least, her plans were set back at least five years. There was no way to make that happen without an even greater crisis. Her head jolted towards the door as it opened and Paulson came in.

"Madam President," he said as he slid into the chair in front of her desk.

"Who said you could sit?"

"No one, but GIS read me in. Did you really think I would simply sit by as you conquered everyone?"

Anna smiled. She sat down, reaching for the bottle of whiskey in her desk. "Would you like one?"

"Sure."

Anna took out two rocks glasses and poured two fingers of whiskey in each. She slid one glass over to Paulson. "Has our asset been discovered?"

Paulson shook his head. "No, ma'am. She's fully recovered and awaiting further instructions." He shifted in his seat. "She did ask about seeing her parents."

"What did you tell her?"

"That I'd look into it."

Anna laughed. "Good thing. They're already dead."

"How?"

"Does it matter?"

"I guess not."

Anna sipped her whiskey. "We need to keep a close eye on Lea McKenna. For me—I mean—us, to succeed, she must be disgraced and out of the picture."

"What do we do?" Paulson asked.

"GIS and I came up with Plan B," Anna said. "Isn't that right, GIS?"

"Affirmative," GIS said over the speakers.

"Sometimes, it sounds different. Like—I don't know," Paulson said.

Anna waved him off. “Never mind that.” She slid a data crystal across her desk. “Here. Transmit this to our friend aboard the *Renault*. It contains her instructions.”

Paulson slipped the crystal into his pocket. “What now?”

“We move ahead with Plan B and destroy that wretched woman.” She walked over to her window overlooking the city. “This is only the beginning. We orchestrated the near destruction of Earth to quickly gain total control over it, but we failed.”

Paulson sipped his whiskey. “Are we done then?”

“No, this is just the beginning,” Anna said.

ABOUT THE AUTHOR

Hi, I'm Steven Atwood. I grew up reading fantasy books and watching science fiction whenever I could. When I was young, I played role-playing games within the fantasy genre. Close to the end of my military career, I started to write. It was something I always wanted to do but never did. I write science fiction and fantasy with a fresh perspective.

Visit my website
http://stevenatwood.net

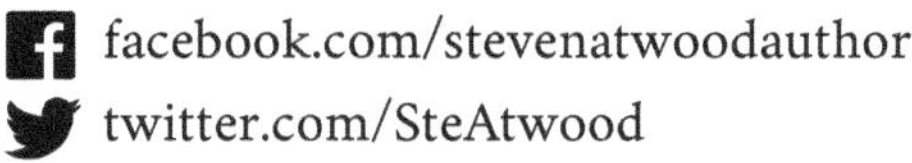

ALSO BY STEVEN ATWOOD

Science Fiction

Cyber Invasion

Amari

Nano WMD

Fantasy

Great Discord Series

Skull of Power

Prophecy of Axain Series

Ravenward

Prophecy of Axain

Iron Fist Keep

Full Circle

Box Sets

Prophecy of Axain Boxset